MOUTH TO MOUTH

A Beach Kingdom Novel

by Tessa Bailey

Copyright © 2018 Tessa Bailey
Print Edition

All rights reserved. No part of this publication may be reproduced, distributed, or transmitted in any form or by any means, including photocopying, recording, or other electronic or mechanical methods, without the prior written permission of the publisher, except in the case of brief quotations embodied in critical reviews and certain other noncommercial uses permitted by copyright law.

TABLE OF CONTENTS

Chapter One	1
Chapter Two	7
Chapter Three	13
Chapter Four	24
Chapter Five	31
Chapter Six	52
Chapter Seven	65
Chapter Eight	74
Chapter Nine	83
Chapter Ten	93
Chapter Eleven	102
Chapter Twelve	115
Chapter Thirteen	122
Chapter Fourteen	130
Chapter Fifteen	146
Chapter Sixteen	161
Chapter Seventeen	174
Excerpt from Runaway Girl	187
Want Access to FREE audiobooks?	195

CHAPTER ONE

God, I fucking hate summer.

Rory Prince shoved the ice pack against his throbbing eye and tried unsuccessfully to tune out the offensive early morning kitchen sounds. The scratching of his oldest brother's pencil across the table might as well have been an air horn pressed directly to the center of his forehead—and was *way* too efficient for nine a.m.

"Do you mind?" Rory muttered. "I'm in recovery mode."

"When are you not?" Andrew didn't even bother to look up from the two clipboards on which he seemed determined to make endless notations. "It's Memorial Day weekend and I have two schedules to organize. Sorry I can't accommodate your hangover." His pencil flew from one set of grids to another. "Where did the black eye come from?"

"Yes, I thought you only gave those out," Rory's other brother, Jamie, said from behind his raised, open book. "Who got the drop on you?"

"Some DFS's," Rory responded, shifting the ice pack, and his brothers hummed in acknowledgment, well aware that DFS stood for *Down for the Summer.* As in, those who didn't live year-round in Long Beach but showed up for three months out of the year to make hell for the residents. "Don't worry, he ended up with two instead of one."

Jamie sighed and finally lowered his worn-in copy of *The*

Grapes of Wrath. "Aren't physical altercations a violation of your probation?"

Rory winked his good eye. "Only if I get caught."

Andrew tossed aside the pencil and flattened both hands on the kitchen table. "All right. I tried to give everyone at least one full day off every week—"

"Jesus, man," Rory deadpanned. "Don't spoil us."

"Look. We've got a bar to run." Andrew massaged his eyes with a forefinger and thumb. Not for the first time, Rory noticed the new lines at the corners and the ice pack started to feel heavier in his hand. "I know it's a lot, lifeguarding during the day and working behind the bar at night. If I could eliminate one of them for us, I would." He dropped his hand. "Things are different than they were four years ago, though. We should be used to it by now."

Things were different? Christ, what an understatement.

Rory, Andrew and Jamie traded long looks over the table, before quickly moving their attention elsewhere. A familiar pit took up residence in Rory's stomach, but he filled it with cement and pasted a bored expression on his face. "Look, all I know is I'm not working Trivia Tuesdays at the bar." He pointed at Jamie. "You herd the nerds this year."

"As long as I can still participate in the quiz while serving drinks."

Rory's lips twitched. "God forbid you miss a chance to blow minds with your bottomless intellect."

Jamie turned the page of his book. "What good is being a genius if I can't make everyone else feel stupid?"

Andrew grabbed their attention with a knuckle rap on the table. "All right, so Jamie, you're on Tuesday nights." Their older brother made a notation on one of his clipboards. "I'm taking

Sunday and Monday because the sports crowd is belligerent and Rory will knock someone out and end up back in a concrete cell—"

"More than likely," Rory drawled, taking a few gulps of black coffee.

"We're all hands on deck Thursday, Friday and Saturday nights—everyone works. So that leaves Wednesday night open." Andrew speared him with a look. "You got it covered?"

"Sure. Wet T-shirt Wednesdays—"

"Nu-uh. Not happening."

Rory smiled at his strait-laced oldest brother to let him know he'd been joking. "I think I've got it, man."

With a nod, Andrew penciled in the final details to the Castle Gate schedule, hoisting it up like Moses probably held the Ten Commandments. "The next three months are going to be crazy, but when things quiet back down in September, we'll have a lot less of Dad's debt to show for it. We're almost there. Play our cards right and this could be the year." He didn't meet their eyes. "Heads down and plow through, okay?" Finally, he ticked a look in both of their directions. "And let me know if anyone asks about him."

Rory swallowed. "Will do."

Jamie set his book down, which was as good as an agreement.

"Next order of business," Andrew started, trading a not-so-subtle glance with Jamie. "Mom's birthday is coming up in a few weeks."

"What do you know?" Rory drawled, his neck itching. "Damn thing rolls around at least once every single year. Same time, too."

"Are you going to come?" Jamie asked, shifting in his chair. "I don't think you realize how much she'd like to see you, Rory."

"You're right, I don't." He laughed without humor and polished off his coffee, softening his tone when his brothers looked disappointed. "I'll let you know, huh?"

Before anyone could respond, the back door of their kitchen opened and Jiya Dalal, the fourth member of their family, breezed in. "Morning, suckers," she murmured, flipping her wave of black hair over her shoulder. "Where's my coffee?"

On cue, Andrew abandoned his almighty clipboards and rose to pour her a cup.

Jiya wasn't technically related, but Rory loved her like a sister. She'd moved with her parents from India to Long Beach the summer before starting fifth grade. One afternoon, Rory and Andrew were playing catch in the backyard—while Jamie read in the shade of their cedar tree—when they noticed a somber brown eye watching them through a hole in the old, rotted fence. That's when the yelling started inside their house. Not just yelling. Angry, vile words meant to cause pain, coming from their father. In those days, their mother responded in kind, too. Before things had escalated.

Slowly, the fence board had slid to one side, revealing a girl Andrew's age, wearing a pink Punjabi suit—although he hadn't known what to call her outfit at the time. She'd waved all three Prince boys through, leading them without words to her garage where they'd watched cartoons on an old television set, Mrs. Dalal bringing them ice-cold Pepsi cans with straws stuck in the top. Jiya's English had only allowed them the most basic communication back then, but eighteen years later, there was only a trace of her accent remaining and she could swear like a goddamn sailor.

Jiya slid over a large metal container from its place of honor on their counter and scooped cumin from its smaller compartment into the pressure cooker where Andrew had already started soaking the ghee to make khichdi, their morning staple ever since Jiya had taken pity on three starving men.

Knowing she would twist his ear like silly putty if he didn't get up to help, Rory stood, breathing through his nose when his brain lurched and smacked off the front of his skull. "Fuck me," he rasped, pinching the bridge of his nose. "I hate summer."

During the rest of the year, Rory worked the bar five nights a week. He made enough money to be comfortable and contribute to the mortgage he shared with his brothers. His customers were regulars. Friends. Locals. As soon as Memorial Day weekend hit, Long Beach transformed into a whole different animal. For one, lifeguarding season began, which meant waking up at the ass crack of dawn. Everyone on the beach was jacked for the time of their life, which meant they acted like idiots—and he couldn't even escape them at the end of the day, since they inevitably showed up at the Castle Gate at night.

"I *love* summertime," Jiya breathed, turning and leaning back against the counter. "My tips at the restaurant triple. By September, I should finally be able to afford the lessons."

As far back as Rory could remember, Jiya had wanted to fly an airplane, but slow season at the restaurant she ran with her parents always seemed to eat into her funds. Every year around this time, she said the same thing. *I should finally be able to afford the lessons.*

Rory glanced over at Andrew to find him staring at Jiya's profile, a frown marring his features. "Hell yeah." He moved around Jiya and elbowed Andrew. "That's great, Ji. Where are you flying us first?"

Andrew handed her a mug of coffee and she breathed in the steam, her dark eyes sparkling. "I'm thinking a pit stop in the

Maldives before we hop over to Australia."

"Count me in," Jamie said, joining them at the counter to grate ginger onto the cutting board. "Let me know when to start packing."

"He'll need three extra suitcases for his books," Rory laughed, then winced when his cranium protested. "Son of a bitch. Today is going to suck."

"There's Advil in my purse."

He almost dove for the leather satchel she'd hung on a chair. "You're an angel."

"True facts." Jiya took an exaggerated breath, set her coffee down and the four of them fell into their usual routine of making breakfast. "What time do you have to be at the Hut?" she asked, referring to the squat, brick headquarters adjacent to the boardwalk where the lifeguards checked in each morning.

"Eleven," Andrew answered, saluting the kitchen in general with the spatula. "Long Beach, your lives are in the hands of the Prince brothers."

Rory dry-swallowed a painkiller. "God help them all."

CHAPTER TWO

THE PRINCE BROTHERS lived, ate, argued and worked two jobs together, so there was no shortage of face time. Hell, they were never *not* in each other's faces. There'd been no formal discussion when deciding that morning not to ride to the Hut as a trio. It had gone unsaid they would find their own way there.

Did they love each other? Yeah. Would they have each other's backs in an alley, even if the odds were three against three hundred? Rory would already be searching the ground for a potential weapon. Did they need some space occasionally? Bet your ass.

While Jamie hopped on the bus, Andrew and Jiya had driven together in his pick-up truck toward the boardwalk. Hoping the late-May breeze would clear the vodka cobwebs from his head, Rory walked, instead of taking his motorcycle. The last-minute decision to hoof it had thrown off his morning routine, resulting in him forgetting his cell phone on the kitchen table, but judging from the packed avenues, he should be thankful he wouldn't have to battle for a parking space with a hangover.

At ten o'clock in the morning, there was already a traffic jam at every intersection, college kids staring at their smartphones at stoplights, the nasal voice of their navigation systems drifting out of the open car windows. A news helicopter circled above, probably feeding footage of the filling beach town back to a local station where a newscaster chirped to the audience. *This Memori-*

al Day weekend is certainly shaping up to be the busiest yet, Bob!

Andrew had been right about the last four years yielding big changes for the Princes. Their mother lived in Bayside, Queens now with her sister. Their father wasn't around anymore. It was just the three of them, back in the house they'd been raised, working to pay bills.

The more things change, the more they stay the same, though, right? The walk down National Boulevard toward the beach felt like it had been recycled from the four previous summers of his life. Wake up after a night of blurry, shit-faced memories, face the guarded disappointment across the kitchen table, while nursing a healthy dose of his own. Fall into the same routine. Beach, bar, bed. Never changing. Never growing or taking on more responsibility. An actor trapped in the reruns of his own life.

What would he do if Andrew asked him to help manage the bar? Or hire and train this year's newest crop of lifeguards? Not that such an occurrence would ever take place, but would he be able to deliver on more, if asked?

Rory was distracted from his thoughts when a blonde walked past him on the sidewalk with her face buried in a book. "Jesus," he muttered. "The female version of Jamie."

When she'd gotten a few feet ahead of Rory, he was powerless to do anything but check out her ass. If there was one perk to summers in Long Beach, it was the abbreviated attire, and this girl was no exception. She wore little, white bun-hugger shorts and flip-flops, gracing Rory with a front row seat to the tight, side-to-side twitch of her backside. It was a superior tush. So superior, he shook out his right hand like it had been burned.

Shame he couldn't see her face. The forward tilt of her head caused short, blonde hair to curtain around her features as she speed walked to the corner, never looking up from her book.

Rory's frown deepened the closer she got to intersection. Traffic might be moving slowly, but the bus lane was wide open and he knew from experience how fast they flew.

"Hey." He cleared his throat and raised his voice. "*Hey.*"

She continued walking, face in book.

"Dammit." Rory gritted his teeth and started to run, not an easy feat considering he'd paired flip-flops with his sweatpants. But he had no choice to sprint, because she was five feet from the crosswalk and showing no signs of slowing down. He caught up with her just as she stepped into the street, wrapping an arm around her waist and yanking her back—

The East Loop bus barreled past blaring its horn.

"*Oh my God.*" She dropped her book—about fucking time—and dug her fingernails into his forearm. "Did that...oh God, that bus almost *hit me.*"

"You couldn't have made it any easier," Rory near-shouted at the top of her head, sounding winded. With her back plastered to his front, Rory could practically feel her shock wear off, giving way to a wave of trembling. He heaved a sigh and lowered his voice. "Consider a switch to audiobooks, huh? Maybe?"

Her head tipped forward, presumably to look at her fallen book. "I didn't like the narrator for this one."

"Enough to get hit by a bus?"

A few beats passed. "If I say yes, will you start shouting again?"

"Yes."

"Then...no?"

Realizing he still held the stranger in a death grip, Rory let her go in degrees to assure himself she was steady. The blonde turned around and blinked up at him through round, red-rimmed eyeglasses—and he experienced the most unexpected twist in his chest. He must have run harder and faster than he thought, because he was winded all over again. On a sucked-in breath, an odd sound escaped his mouth. A scrape of noise. What the hell?

This girl. She was fucking…*amazing.* She reminded him of a little sunbeam with summer-kissed skin and big features, especially those dove-gray eyes. Oh *fuck.* Her lips. They were parted slightly and inviting, the sun bathing them in a sheen.

Forget what he'd said about her being the female version of Jamie.

"Whoa," she whispered.

Tell me about it. "What's your name?"

If her widened eyes meant she was surprised by the sudden drop in his voice, she wasn't the only one. "I'm Olive. Cunningham."

"Olive." For some reason, color climbed her neck when he said her name. "I'm Rory Prince."

"Hi." She smacked a hand to her forehead. "And duh. *Thank you.* For saving me from being road kill. If I had to die horrifically, I would have chosen a different book to be my last."

Rory stooped down and picked up the fallen tome, making no effort to hide his perusal of her bare legs on the way back up. They were covered in goose bumps. "You're making it sound like you hate this book…" he said, stepping close until she tilted her head back to maintain eye contact. "But you were lost in another world reading it."

"I get lost in magazines at the dentist office." He heard her swallow. "I just have a thing for words."

"What else do you have a thing for?"

"Probably other stuff," she whispered. "But I'm having trouble thinking of them right this second."

"Why is that?"

"I almost got hit by a bus." She jerked a thumb over her shoulder. "Did you miss that?"

Rory couldn't stop his grin. "Oh, I caught it." Up ahead, he could hear the ocean and knew he needed to be at work. He would let down Andrew at some point this summer, no need to make it on the first day. But *this girl*. He was just supposed to walk away?

His grin faded. "I have to be at work soon. I'm lifeguarding today and we start at eleven. But I have a few minutes before I have to run." He forced a concerned expression onto his face. "You look shaken up, sunbeam. We should probably get you a coffee and my number."

A laugh burst out of her, loud enough to turn heads on the sidewalk. She slapped her hands over her mouth but continued to giggle behind them. The sound was so contagious, his own low rumble joined it and he couldn't help but think, *there's never been a morning like this. There's nothing even remotely recycled about this.*

"I'm actually meeting a girlfriend," Olive said finally. "It's a study date."

"I have great news. No one studies during the summer time."

"I do." With a smile that showed off the slight gap between her two front teeth, she pushed her glasses higher on her nose. "At the risk of sounding like a huge nerd, I'm taking a summer class at Stony Brook. I'm going to be a psychology major there in the fall and I want to be familiar with the course materials. And okay…" She blushed to her hairline. "I didn't risk sounding like a huge nerd. That was full-on dweeb."

Even though her enthusiasm was adorable, Rory encountered a kick of unease. He'd never been in a serious relationship, but he'd gone out with a lot of different kinds of girls…*once*. There wasn't much that could intimidate him. He'd grown up poor and served hard time. But people with book smarts? Yeah, he had the look memorized. *That* look. The one that said they pegged him as being uneducated with nothing in his future but answering to someone else and making a working man's salary for it.

On those extremely rare occasions Rory spent time with a book-smart girl, he didn't really give a shit when she gave him the look. The one that said, I'm going to enjoy tonight and never tell a single one of my friends about it. What did he care? He wasn't exactly planning on telling anyone, either. It was just a basic need being met. A diversion.

Olive didn't seem like a diversion. Not even a little bit.

He *really* didn't want her to give him the look.

"Uh, right." Rory winked at Olive, handed her the book and backed in the direction of the beach. "Look, no more walking without looking where you're going, all right, sunbeam?"

Her smile dropped.

"Don't study too hard," he said, punching the crosswalk button. Damn, walking away from a girl wasn't supposed to be hard, was it? His stomach felt like two stones grinding together. When he glanced back, Olive took a step toward him, then changed her mind and retreated. With a weird tightening in his throat, Rory faced the street again. The light changed and Rory started to cross—

"*Wait!*"

CHAPTER THREE

TOO BAD YOU couldn't edit real life.

Because she'd definitely just yelled, "*Wait!*"

At the hottest guy she'd ever seen in person. A hot guy who'd *saved her life*.

Good thing she'd sounded extra desperate.

Olive Cunningham tried not to cringe at the note of desperation hanging in the warm summer air and watched Rory slow to a stop, glancing back at her over his muscular shoulder. Wariness danced in eyes she knew were translucent green and hardened the strong lines of his back, reminding her of an unbroken stallion. What had she said to make him throw up his guard? Olive was positive it could have been any number of things. Having been home schooled straight through the twelfth grade, her experience with the opposite sex was limited to neighborhood boys and the ones she read about in books.

When it came time for her to start dating, she'd envisioned herself with a starter boyfriend. Someone non-threatening and endearingly awkward who was still developing the fashion sense that would stay with him throughout adulthood. Rory was the least awkward human being she'd ever encountered. His dark brown hair was finger brushed and somehow perfect, offset by his cut jaw and the beginning shadow of scruff. He was smooth and he lived inside his skin like a worn-in pair of jeans. Not a starter boyfriend. Not a boy anything.

Sexual, bold, protective, funny. A man.

A man with a black eye. And like, twenty-six tattoos, not that she'd tried to count.

His sigh carried on the breeze as he returned to the sidewalk, planting his big hands on narrow hips. "Yeah, sunbeam?"

Don't just stand here and moon over him giving you a nickname. Think fast. "Public access television," she blurted. "Rainstorms, Sting, calligraphy…milkshakes."

He raised a dark eyebrow.

"You asked me what else I have a thing for," Olive explained, clutching the book to her chest. When his mouth spread into a smile, she realized he had full, beautiful lips. Attached to his angular face, they made him look like an angel who'd spent some time in hell.

"Sting? Isn't he a little before your time?"

"That's the great thing about music. When you discover it for the first time, it might as well be brand new." Since he didn't seem inclined to come any closer, even though they'd practically kissed a few minutes ago, Olive braved up and took a few steps in Rory's direction. Watched him plant his tongue against the inside of his cheek and breathe slowly. "If I ask what *you* have a thing for, will I regret it?"

Rory didn't respond. He was probably wondering why some random chick was on a mission to make him late for work. Honestly, she was pretty impressed by her own bravery. She'd only been living on her own in Long Beach for a week. In that time, she'd learned all about ordering takeout online, assembled a butt load of furniture and explored enough of the town to go out for a walk without getting lost. Apparently she hadn't quite conquered the ability to avoid death by speeding bus. *Baby steps.*

Everything she'd done since arriving from Oklahoma had

seemed small. A tiny tick toward being a fully independent adult, out from under the thumb of her parents. Maybe they'd been more like leaps, though, because she was definitely flirting a little bit with a sexy lifeguard with no clue if she was doing it correctly.

The longer Rory went without answering, though, the more her confidence started to wane. She wasn't his type. He had a girlfriend. She'd shown too much interest. It could have been any number of things that made him back off. Best to chalk this conversation up to a practice run and go back to reading. While stationary this time.

"Okay, um..." She shrugged her left shoulder. "Have a good day at work. Thanks again for preventing my early demise..."

Olive trailed off as Rory relieved her of the book, tucked it under his arm and presented his hand. "Milkshakes, right? I got you."

"Wait. What?"

"We're going to get a milkshake." They both watched closely as he wove their fingers together and sparks tickled the length of Olive's arm. "And I'm carrying your books for you while we talk about Sting. We've been transported back to another time and place."

"Aren't you going to be late for work?"

"We'll drink fast. Come on."

Just like that, Olive Cunningham of Muskogee, Oklahoma was being pulled along National Boulevard by a man who oozed excitement...and some definite danger. Shouldn't she be more cautious? Yes. Certainly. But why would this man save her life only to kill her? He'd been the one to walk away, too. She'd called him back. Surely it wouldn't hurt to have a milkshake with him in public in broad daylight.

Reassured, Olive allowed her own excitement to take flight.

She watched the flex of his back and triceps as they walked, puzzled over the speculative glances he threw at her over his shoulder. Overall, though, she was relieved they hadn't parted ways back at the intersection. Something told her she wouldn't have put Rory from her mind easily at all.

They had only been walking for a few minutes when Rory pulled Olive to a stop in front of Mike's Shakes. As she'd seen earlier during her internet search, the old-fashioned sign was faded, the windows were wallpapered in advertisements for local music gigs and milkshake specials. Rory opened the door to the sound of a tinkling bell, as if escorting her into a palace.

"After you."

"Thanks," she murmured, passing beneath his arm and feeling his breath on her temple. "Th-this is actually where I'm meeting my study date."

"Yeah?"

She hummed. "It's my first time here, though."

As always, when about to try something new or perform an out-of-the-ordinary activity, Olive heard her mother's voice in her ear. *Hello, YouTubers! Today we're at Mike's Milkshakes celebrating three million subscribers. Comment down below with your favorite milkshake flavor! Don't forget to hit the like button.*

Olive gave a rapid headshake, trying to jostle the voice free. How long would she turn even the most basic event into a YouTube video?

Rory, still holding her hand, led her to one of the few booths positioned in front of the window, sliding into the booth beside her. On the same side. He stretched his arm along the back of the seat as easy as breathing, and within those close quarters, his scent hit her stronger than it had outside. Menthol shaving cream, coffee, the faint smell of something sharp.

"At least wait until after we order to sniff me."

"Oh God." She faced forward in a snap. "I didn't realize I was doing it."

The tan column of his neck flexed as he laughed. "My turn now," he said, sobering, leaning in. "Fair is fair."

The tip of Rory's nose grazed her neck and Olive's thighs audibly smacked together, squeezing, her lips popping open on a gasp as he breathed deeply in the space above her pulse. What was happening to her? Had this man reached inside her and found an on switch for her sex drive? As recently as this morning, she'd almost had to talk herself into being horny and exploring her urges, because grown women were *supposed* to be. Thoughts, fantasies, book scenes inspired her. Never someone in the flesh. Live and in person.

Rory pulled back and locked glazed eyes on her, their mouths mere inches apart. "Jesus Christ. Barely touched you. Wonder what that body would do if I got my hands and mouth on it?"

Faster than lightning, the seam of Olive's shorts became damp, uncomfortable. Rory's breaths came faster against her lips. They were going to kiss, right here in this milkshake shop—and even with precious little kissing experience, she wondered if they'd be able to stop.

"All right, you two," the waiter groused from behind Rory. "Ain't it a little early for this?"

Rory's expression went from hot to cold so fast, Olive shivered. A muscle jumped in his cheek as he sat up straighter and slowly turned to face the waiter, hitting him with a stony look. "I don't know." His long fingers flexed on the table top, his fist coming down hard on the surface. *Whap.* "Is it?"

The waiter was suddenly fascinated by his order pad. "It's all good, man. Sorry. What can I bring you?"

Another handful of seconds passed before Rory answered, the tension building further in the small restaurant. "Whatever your three most popular flavors are," he said in a low voice. "We'll take those."

"You got it."

Olive didn't realize she'd been holding her breath until the waiter loped off, disappearing through the swinging doors into the kitchen. She let it out silently, her awareness of Rory's air of danger bigger and more unavoidable than before. What in the world had just happened? This man who'd pulled her out of the path of oncoming traffic seemed capable of mowing people down just as handily. As if reading her mind, Rory shook his head. "You're one of the smart ones, Olive," he said, pronouncing smart like *smahht*. "You weren't supposed to call me back."

Her pulse skipped as she processed that. "You were trying to protect me from yourself?" He searched her face but didn't answer. "Do I need protecting?"

"*God*, no, sunbeam. Not from me," he rasped, frustration shifting his body in the seat. "Look, you asked me if you'd regret it. Finding out what I have a thing for. The answer is yes." He tilted his face toward the light, giving her a better view of his damaged eye. "Ask me how I got this."

It was so hard not to follow that command, considering she'd been dying to know the source of his injury since they'd crossed paths. She didn't want to hear the answer now, though. Not when he clearly thought it was going to be a deal breaker. "Why don't you just tell me when you're ready?"

That caught him off guard, but he recovered fast. "I was out being a fucking idiot. Looking for…" He trailed off, as if surprised by his own words. "I *look* for the fights. I go out and find them."

"Why?"

"I don't know." He tapped a fist on the table. "And it doesn't matter. You shouldn't be around it. You're the type of girl who'd realize it sooner than later, so I beat you to the punch." The expression he turned on her was almost accusatory. "Turns out, it's not that easy to walk away from you."

The waiter appeared at the side of the table with a tray, moving their milkshake trio one by one in front of them and setting down straws. In Olive's periphery, she could see the waiter hovering as if wanting to ask if they needed anything else, but she couldn't manage to rip her attention off of Rory and the waiter eventually left. "I didn't want you to walk away."

He laughed under his breath. "You going to be trouble for me, sunbeam?"

"Why don't we just drink milkshakes?"

Still looking troubled, Rory unwrapped three straws and stuck them into their own respective milkshakes. "Okay, let's pick our favorite. You first."

"Wait, no." Olive's spine went ramrod straight. "This feels way too much like a YouTube channel challenge."

"I don't know what any of that means, but it sounds serious."

"Oh, you have no idea. Subscribers hang in the balance." When his confusion demanded an explanation, she blew out a long breath. "I moved here from Oklahoma a week ago."

"That explains the cute accent."

"I don't have an accent. You do."

"Agree to disagree." He picked up the chocolate milkshake, his fingers sliding through the condensation on the glass as he gripped it, held the straw to her bottom lip. "Taste, Olive."

Her thighs threatened to smack together again, but she narrowly avoided the action, drinking deeply of the thick, delicious shake, rich cocoa waking up her taste buds and making them sing. All the while, Rory's gaze tracked a path from her lips to the hollow of her throat and back. "It's amazing," she managed, letting the straw go. "And this is nothing like a challenge."

"Good." He set the shake down with a smirk. "I think."

Olive picked up the next shake—mint chip—took a sip and handed it to Rory, so he could do the same. "If you know nothing about the YouTube world, this is all going to sound utterly crazy. But here goes. When I was thirteen, my parents started a YouTube channel. Meet the Cunninghams. They filmed me and my siblings doing everything, during most of our waking hours. Getting ready for school, eating in restaurants, making slime—"

"What? Why?"

"It's a thing." Knowing uncomfortable feelings were about to surround her like cloud cover, she swapped mint chip back for classic chocolate. "People watch. Every day. They subscribe to our family." She ran her finger vertically through the fogged glass. "But it's the sitcom curse, you know? When kids hit a certain age, they kind of run their course. So the videos became mostly about my little brother and sister, Henderson and Pearl." She forced a smile onto her face. "Eight million subscribers at last count, though. That's…really impressive."

Rory had been sitting with the straw poised in front of his mouth for her entire explanation. "You said they filmed most of your waking hours. After they took you out of the picture, they kept filming your brother and sister?"

"Yes."

"If you weren't in the videos anymore, where did you go?"

Oh wow. She'd severely underestimated what it would be like to tell someone out loud that she'd essentially been fired from her own family for getting older. "In my room." She reached for the third shake—ugh, pina colada? *Really?* "I stayed out of the way."

"And they let you? They *wanted* that?" Her silence served as an affirmative and Rory's outrage was palpable. "That's extremely fucked up, sunbeam."

"It is, a little." She sipped the pina colada even though it was gross. "Maybe a lot."

He leaned in and pressed his lips to her cheek. "They shouldn't have done that to you. I met you fifteen minutes ago and I know you don't deserve that."

"Thanks," she whispered, trying not to be obvious about inhaling shaving cream smell.

"That must have been a while ago…right?" Rory asked, pulling back and narrowing his eyes. "You said you've been here a week. Where were you before Long Beach?"

"Living with my parents."

He set down the milkshake slowly. "Hold up, Olive. How old are you?"

Uh oh. Was this going to be an issue? "Eighteen."

"Christ." He dragged both hands down his face. "That's young."

Olive reared back. "I'm renting my own apartment. My shower curtain matches my towels. There are serious adult decisions being made here." Her comeback earned her a quirked male smile and she couldn't help but return it. "How old are you?"

"Twenty-four." He seemed to be chewing glass. "How do you have your own place at eighteen? Long Beach isn't cheap, especially in the summer time."

She hesitated a moment. "The thing about eight million subscribers…it means advertisers will pay a ton to run ads on your channel…"

He leaned away. "So you're not only young and smart, you're a rich girl."

"Hey, I earned it," she deadpanned. "Sliming ain't easy."

"Olive," he groaned. "Please stop being so fucking cute."

Her stomach flipped. "Because you still want to walk away?"

"I shouldn't have to. You should be running toward something better." Rory's expression was the epitome of conflicted, but he was saved from having to elaborate when the bell dinged over the door and a girl Olive recognized walked into Mike's Shakes. She looked around at the ancient décor and made a face, hefting her backpack higher on her shoulders. When Leanne spotted her, she waved. Olive's arm felt like lead, but she managed to lift it and return the greeting.

"Oh, um. My study date is here."

Rory hadn't glanced once at the newcomer, continuing to study her face. "I have to get to work, anyway."

"Okay," she murmured, reaching into her pocket for money. "Let me help pay—"

He caught her wrist. "On me, sunbeam."

Leanne slid into the booth across from them slowly and Olive didn't even need to glance over to know her study partner was watching with rapt interest. "H-hey Olive. I brought the Perspectives and Connections book you left in my car on Thursday."

"Thank you."

"Perspectives and Connections," mouthed Rory with a wry twist of his lips. "I'll leave you to it."

Olive felt like she'd walked into a sub-zero freezer as Rory rose from the booth and tossed some bills on the table. He took one long final look at her and moved in a slow swagger toward the exit. And she couldn't yell *wait* this time. Not if she wanted to maintain one ounce of self-respect. Instead, she turned in the booth and faced Leanne, trying desperately to swallow the lump in her throat. "So, um…where did we leave off last time? I think it was the—"

Rory appeared to her left. "I left my phone at home. Write down your number," he said, pronouncing it *numba*.

"Who leaves their phone?" Leanne mused, playing with her own device.

But Olive barely heard her over the sudden palpitations happening in her chest. By some feat of willpower, she managed not to break into song. She signaled Leanne for a pen and wrote her cell number on a straw wrapper, sliding it toward Rory. "Are you going to use it?"

He left without answering.

Olive smiled through the entire study session.

He'd call.

He'd *totally* call.

CHAPTER FOUR

No way Rory could call her.

If he called Olive, he'd arrange a time to see her again. If he saw her again, once wouldn't be enough. Time had stood still from the moment he pulled her out of the bus's path, right up until he finally left Mike's Shakes with her number in his pocket. Everything had taken a back seat to what she said next, how she moved, smelled, laughed.

He sat on a bench in the Hut's locker room now, staring down at the ripped straw wrapper, smoothing out the curled ends on his thigh. Around him, the locker room moved in ripples of animated color, the other lifeguards excited to kick off the summer season, already making plans to hit the boardwalk bars tonight. Lockers slammed, cell phones dinged, playful insults rang out.

Meanwhile Rory was transfixed by ten digits on a narrow strip of white paper. She'd drawn smiley faces in her zeroes, which was just further proof calling the number was a bad idea. And yet. If he hadn't left his phone at home, he would have already texted her.

There had been an unusual tug in his gut the entire time and it was more than him being turned on. He'd wanted to sit her in his lap and feed her milkshakes and find out what caused all her different smiles. The teasing one was his favorite by far. The one that challenged him to stop being so serious.

Funny enough, serious wasn't Rory's thing. Definitely not when it came to women. He was a temporary thrill—and it went both ways. Yet he'd found himself…exposed in front of Olive. More than once. And she'd barely pushed. His guard had dropped itself before he knew what happened. Would he take back those moments if he could?

No. No, he wouldn't change a single thing about that morning.

An elbow caught him in the side and Rory lifted his head to find Jamie sitting beside him. How long had his brother been there? "Hey."

Jamie eyeballed the straw wrapper. "Eventful walk to work?"

Rory sighed and dragged a hand through his hair. "You could say that."

"She smiley faced her zeroes."

"Yeah."

They sat in silence for a moment.

"You going to call her?" Jamie prompted, beginning to dig through his backpack.

Rory stood, dropped the phone number onto the top shelf of his open locker and stripping off his shirt. "Nope."

"That sounds pretty definitive."

"Has to be."

"Why?"

Off came the sweatpants, leaving Rory in his red, standard-issue lifeguard trunks. "She's eighteen." When Jamie winced, Rory made a sound of agreement. "That's only the beginning. She's a smart girl. College coming up. I'm not going to let her waste time on me."

Jamie's brows snapped together. "I'd say you're not a waste of time, but you wouldn't believe me."

"She doesn't even know I've done time." His chest knotted thinking of how she'd react. Part of Rory wished he'd told her, just so he wouldn't have to speculate forever what she might have said. "It was just a crazy, one-time thing. Nothing happened. We drank milkshakes."

"Since when do your crazy one-time things involve milkshakes?"

"Since this morning, okay?" Rory shot back, pounding a fist into his locker. "Drop it."

Jamie adopted his signature cocky pose. Arms crossed, expression bored. "I'll drop it when you throw her number in the trash."

Rory laughed and shook his head. "You *prick*."

"Can't do it, can you?"

Not a hope in hell. "Why is this such a big deal to you?"

Jamie lost a degree of smugness. "Look, we're all busy during the year. I'm teaching, Andrew never leaves the bar." He shrugged a shoulder. "We see each other at home, but we're not around each other non-stop, like we are in the summer. And every time Memorial Day weekend rolls around, you're a little less…optimistic. About yourself. About everything."

The back of Rory's neck pinched tight and he rolled the muscles to loosen them. "Are you sure you're an economics teacher and not a counselor?"

"Positive. How well do you think I'd handle adolescent feelings?"

"Not well."

"No shit." Jamie tipped his chin toward the top shelf of Rory's locker. "And speaking of adolescents."

"Fuck you."

His brother grinned, but it was short lived. "You said she's smart?"

Rory swallowed and snatched the whistle out of his locker, dropping it over his head. "Yeah," he rasped.

"Then she had a reason for sliding you her digits. Maybe give her a little more credit."

He considered Jamie's words for all of a second before disregarding them. "You can be smart and still be naïve. I'm doing her a favor." His fingers paused in the process of engaging his Master lock. "I'm sitting there talking to her and my fucking eye is killing me from last night. I'm wondering if she smells the vodka coming out of my pores. And she's so...fresh. And *better*. The waiter looks at me sideways this morning and I can't—I *couldn't* stop myself from getting pissed. Showing her exactly what I am. It wouldn't work, Jamie." A vision of Olive pushing up her glasses drifted into his conscience and stung him. "We only spent an hour together and I know it's crazy, but if I went out with her, I'd want her to be...mine. *Think* about that. Some fucking ex-con locking down this young girl with a successful future her first summer out of her parents' house. No matter how you slice it, I end up the villain. I don't want to be her villain."

Jamie opened his mouth to respond, but he was interrupted by the door to the Hut flying open and rebounding off a row of lockers with an earsplitting rattle.

"I'm here, cocksuckers."

Marcus "Diesel" O'Shaughnessy stood outlined in the doorway. All shirtless, six foot five inches of him. He swaggered into the Hut, stopping to high-five lifeguards and show off the new naked lady tattoo on his arm to everyone he passed.

"For chrissakes," Jamie muttered. "I'd almost forgotten about this asshole."

"Nope. Turns up every year like a bad penny." Rory slid his

brother a side glance. "You let me know if he says something stupid to you, all right?"

A muscle flexed in Jamie's cheek. "He's a loudmouth, but he's mostly harmless." He shoved Rory off balance with his shoulder. "You have to stop fighting my battles for me—we know how that ends." Jamie gave him a pointed look. "I can fight them myself."

"Right." Rory let the subtle reminder of his incarceration roll off his shoulder. "You going to smother him with your book collection?"

Jamie let his locker door swing open, revealing a neat row of novels. "I came prepared."

Rory was still shaking his head when Marcus reached them, rolling to a stop like a goddamn tank and wrapping an arm around Jamie's shoulders. "Ahhh, and who's this hiding over here? How the hell are you, Jamie Prince?" He only laughed when Jamie muttered "please fuck off" under his breath. "Come on, man. I know you missed me." He let go of Jamie, stepped back and flexed, creating the human version of a field goal. "Where else do you get quality eye candy like this? It's got to be *amazing* for you to have me around."

Jamie blew out at breath at the ceiling. "Marcus, don't make me suggest the quiet game this early in the summer."

Marcus pointed at him and grinned. "I'm going to win this time."

"You never win."

Even though he was trying to heed Jamie's request to back off, Rory couldn't help listening carefully to every word that came out of Marcus's mouth, waiting for him to slip up and say something out of line. This kind of needling was par for the course with the oversized gym rat. He had a big mouth—and for some strange reason, he was always running it around Jamie. If it was anyone else giving Jamie a hard time, Rory wouldn't be able to stop himself from stepping in, but Marcus genuinely seemed to like Jamie, though they were exact opposites. Insinuating that Jamie must be thrilled to ogle him, on account of Jamie being gay, was a bad assumption. And kind of offensive. Except it had become obvious over the course of several summers that Marcus had no clue his bullshit came off as rude. Still, why Jamie tolerated it, Rory had no idea.

"I have some great news for you, Jamie Prince," Marcus continued, stripping off his sweatpants and tossing them haphazardly into his open locker. "Andrew hired me as security at the Castle Gate this summer. To check IDs and shit. I'm a bouncer now, son."

"And today in self-fulfilling prophecies…" Jamie muttered.

"You don't have to be away from me a single second." Marcus pulled his red lifeguard shorts on over his briefs, not-too-subtly adjusting his junk. "Lucky you."

"I'm ecstatic," Jamie deadpanned, looping his whistle around his head. "I'm heading to my chair."

"Hold on, I'll walk with you," Marcus said, rushing to grab his gear. "I need some, ah…practice. Acting as a security guard."

Rory couldn't help but laugh as Jamie staunchly ignored Marcus and bee-lined for the exit, forcing Marcus to lope after him in one flip-flop, the other in his gargantuan paw.

Now that Rory was alone, the straw wrapper almost glowed from its position on the top shelf of his locker. Closing the door and leaving it there felt symbolic. That's exactly what needed to be done with Olive. He needed to shut the door on the connection they'd made this morning and leave this funny, fresh-faced girl with a future alone. No calling her. No dating her. No searching out her face on the beach.

He didn't expect her to search him out instead. In the most unconventional way.

CHAPTER FIVE

OLIVE HEAVED A satisfied breath when she saw an open spot on the beach. Memorial Day weekend in Long Beach was pure insanity, and she thanked God her apartment was close enough to walk. Cars were in a dead gridlock around the town, parking spots being fought over like dogs with a bone. Frankly, the atmosphere of competitive relaxation was kind of intimidating, but she hadn't been to the actual beach since moving in, and the incredible weather demanded she leave her studying behind and bask in the sunshine.

It was Saturday, a perfectly acceptable day to be selfish. She would make up for neglecting her school work later and she'd have tan lines as a bonus.

I have great news. No one studies during the summertime.

Rory's voice drifted down from the blue sky and she sighed. Since meeting him yesterday, snippets of their conversation seemed to find her at the oddest times. Like when she was using her vibrator on the highest setting last night and remembered him saying, *Jesus Christ. Barely touched you. Wonder what that body would do if I got my hands and mouth on it?*

See? The oddest times.

Olive snuck into the sliver of space and plunked down her beach bag. She rolled out her favorite towel, which was a headshot of Sigmund Freud above the words "Your Mom." After making sure there wasn't a single wrinkle in the towel, she sat down in the very center and applied sunscreen…beneath her cover up.

It wasn't that she didn't like her boobs. It was that she *hated* her boobs. And even though she knew logically no one on the beach would pay them any attention, as soon as she removed the gauzy white top that skimmed her thighs, her brain would lie to her, whispering that *everyone* was staring at her rack. Thanks to homeschooling, she'd never been forced to walk down a high school hallway full of peers with her body's changes on display. Once when Olive was fifteen, however, a neighborhood guy her age had been helping his mother carry groceries into the house. When he saw Olive waving across the street, he held two cantaloupes in front of his chest and called, "Hey, look. It's Olive and her huge knockers."

She'd gone inside immediately and performed enough Internet research to know that her bust was above average in size and was properly horrified. And without her mother to confide in about her self-consciousness, she'd remained in that state for roughly three years. Now here she was, about to unveil her melons to the masses.

Maybe she *should* have stayed home with her books. They were her solace—and that's why she studied during the summertime and took bonus classes. She enjoyed it. When her parents asked her to take a step back from *Meet the Cunninghams*, she'd needed a distraction from the hurt. School work had been the easiest way to continue being productive without a camera on her. Not to mention, she'd had an ulterior motive in focusing on her grades. She'd hoped to win back her parents' approval, but in the midst of YouTube glory, it had only been fleeting. *Keep up the good work, Olive.* Then back to their regularly scheduled program.

Words on the page was where she snuggled up at night,

whether they told tales of historical events, mathematics or dystopian futures with romance thrown in for good measure. She loved all of the words. Every single one.

During her senior year of high school, she'd taken psychology as an elective and found herself fascinated by the different philosophies of thought. She'd had so many feelings about being placed in the opposite corner than her family, giving those feelings a more scientific term, such as *separation anxiety* had helped. She wasn't just lonely, she was having the appropriate emotional response to isolation. It was right there in her textbooks and it helped to give that emptiness a name. Applying for colleges and choosing psych as her major had been a no-brainer. Why wouldn't she want to help others deal with the same issues in the future? In the meantime, she would continue to deal with them herself.

She was still far from overcoming them.

Up until now, Olive had somehow managed to avoid looking at the closest lifeguard tower, but she did so now—and deflated when the guy sitting in the chair didn't even resemble Rory a little bit. Although she wasn't sure if it was in relief or disappointment.

There was one thing she did know. She wasn't going to sit around waiting for him to call. Or replaying their morning together and wondering if she could have done something differently. For years, she'd played that *what if* game with her family and it was a new day. A new day of matching shower curtains and towels, dammit.

That burst of pride turned out to be exactly what Olive needed to remove her cover-up. She whipped it off and stuffed it into her beach bag. There. Done. She'd inflicted her breasts on the beach and they'd just have to deal. Tan lines or bust.

Olive placed her glasses carefully in her bag's front pocket and flopped down on her back, dug her heels into the granules of sand and cleared her mind of insecurities and what ifs, letting the sun's heat bake them away. Salsa music reached her ears from one side, rap music from the other. The beach goers were jovial, calling to each other, their voices dripping with Long Island. Kids squealed down at the water line and occasionally kicked sand onto Olive as they ran past. The chaos somehow took place around her without involving her, though, leaving her to bask in anonymity, the heat nearly putting her to sleep.

She wasn't sure what caused her eyes to pop open. Or what caused a pinwheel to roll down her spine. Something made her sit up, though, fanning herself with a hand to cool her sun-warmed skin. Without fail, her attention drifted to the lifeguard station—and there he was.

Rory leaned forward in the elevated chair, his hands clasped loosely between his knees, watching her behind a pair of black sunglasses. Yes, there was no doubt he watched her, a muscle ticking in his cheek. The tattoos hadn't been fully visible the day before, but they were on full display now, hugging big portions of his skin like spiderwebs. And Olive might as well have been naked for the awareness that crept over her, lifting goose bumps down the length of her arms, making her thighs feel like gelatin, all the way up to her sex. When had he gotten there? How long had he been watching her? How did he reach out and touch her from thirty yards away?

Olive turned back around to face the water, forcing her fingers to stop clutching the sides of the towel. He hadn't even waved. Or smiled. He almost looked mad at her, which made no sense, since he'd been the one to *not* call. What would a cool, calm and collected adult with a new Bed Bath & Beyond credit card do in this situation? Olive had no clue, but if she sat there much longer, she was going to melt under his close scrutiny.

Reminding herself that no one cared about her boobs, Olive stood up, wincing when she had no choice to dust some stray sand off her butt, and walked casually toward the water. Really, she'd been planning to go for a swim at some point. She'd never even dipped a toe into the Atlantic Ocean, so now was a good a time as any.

"Oh my God," she croaked when icy cold water rushed up her ankles and licked at her knees. "It's eighty degrees. Shouldn't you be warm?"

There was no choice but to wade in farther after coming this far. It hurt, though. She wanted to be back on top of Sigmund Freud cultivating a tan, not courting hypothermia.

Olive heard her whining conscience and frowned at the horizon. She'd left the comfort of her parents' mini-mansion—complete with *heated* pool—to make a real change. They could cast her aside in the name of Internet fame, but *she'd* made the decision to leave Oklahoma for New York. She'd taken control of the separation this time, so they couldn't do it for her. Now that she was on her own in this big, unfamiliar place, she wouldn't stay stuck in a bedroom listening to life take place on the other side of her door.

She took a deep breath, whimpered under her breath, and let her body drop beneath the surface of the water. It covered her head with a rushing foam gurgle, before the world around her turned muted. Bluish green pushed against her lids, allowing her to see the color even with her eyes closed. It was such a glorious and beautiful rush, she forgot to be cold. When she emerged from the surface again, she couldn't contain the laugh that bubbled up in her throat. Totally worth leaving her books to gather dust for the afternoon.

Kids on top of boogie boards were carried toward the shore by waves. They were probably half her age, so she had zero reservations about freestyle swimming farther into the murky blue, letting the sounds of the shore recede, stopping only when her feet could no longer touch sand. After a few minutes of letting herself drift, she decided to swim back to shore, march right up to Rory and...force him into a pleasant conversation. Yup. *That* would show him. He might have lamented their age gap, but she'd prove being young didn't amount to being immature.

With that plan in mind, Olive let a wave crest over her and started to kick. She couldn't seem to make any progress toward shore, though. Her position never changed, only shifting her sideways...or farther out. Was she drifting farther out?

That's when she heard a whistle pierce the afternoon air—and she knew it was for her.

"Oh God. No, no, no...this isn't happening." She swam as hard as she could, losing steam after about ten seconds and attempting to reach the bottom of the ocean floor with her toes. She didn't even scrape it. She did, however, become very aware of a separate current running down near her feet. Undertow. Unbelievable. She'd gotten stuck in an undertow.

A wave broke over Olive's head, but not before she made out the blurry figure cutting toward her in the water at a fast clip, a red flotation device dragging along the surface behind him. Her lack of glasses prevented her from making out exact details—and then she couldn't see anything. A healthy dose of water was sucked up through her nose when she tried to breathe. Panic made her flail, even though she knew it would burn energy. She couldn't stop. Couldn't stop trying to remain on the surface where the oxygen lived. *I'm drowning. I'm going to drown. Why did I leave my books? They've been so good to me.*

An arm wrapped around her chest and she instinctively tried to fight the restriction, thinking it would drag her farther down. She twisted, her vision nothing but blurred blues and greens, fear roaring in her ears.

"I've got you, sunbeam. *Easy.* I'm here to help you."

The imploring voice near her ear ceased her struggles immediately. Rory. That's right. It was Rory, not some angry sea monster hell bent on drowning her. Within seconds, he had her face up, the flotation device pressed securely to her chest.

"Hold onto this while I get you back to shore. Wrap your arms around it. Good girl." Was it her imagination or did he brush a kiss over her hair? "*Goddammit,*" he rasped, starting to swim. "Didn't you hear me whistling? You just kept…I saw you go under…"

If Olive wasn't totally spent after battling the sea gods, she would have said something to comfort Rory. He sounded so upset. But coming down from her adrenaline surge and landing in a pile of relief made her almost drowsy, so she could only listen, realizing absently that Rory had been required to save her life *twice* in twenty-four hours.

How humiliating.

Even more embarrassing was how fast they reached the shore after she'd been unable to swim an inch in the same direction. Her feet slid backward in the sand and then she was hoisted into Rory's arms, the top of her head finding a home under his chin without conscious thought. They were surrounded by an applauding crowd as Rory walked them up the beach, and the tension in his shoulders told Olive he didn't like the attention they were getting.

"Talk to me," he said, leaning down to search her eyes. "I got to you in time. Right? Look, I just really need you to talk to me."

Which one of them was shaking? "I'm fine. I'm just cold."

"Cold. Okay." Seeming relieved that he had a problem to work on, Rory picked up the pace to a stride, leaving their audience in the dust. Water dripped off the ends of his hair and coasted down his shoulder, chest, jaw, dripping onto Olive, but she didn't mind it one bit, because a couple of drips was easily better than a whole ocean. Also the droplets had been warmed on Rory's skin before landing on hers and there was something grounding about that. Like he was resuscitating her without trying.

His worried expression drifted in and out of the sunlight, keeping his face mostly in the shadows, but occasionally she would get a peek at the set jaw, downward slashing eyebrows. He was on a mission to take her somewhere, but until he unlocked a door and carried her inside a dark locker room, she didn't speculate on where.

"This is the Hut," he murmured, adjusting his hold to bring Olive tighter against his chest as they passed through long rows of lockers, a slim, wooden bench running down the middle. "I'm going to catch hell for leaving the beach, but I just need to get you warmed up, sunbeam. You won't stop shaking."

"You either."

She heard him swallow. "I don't know what you're talking about."

Olive decided to let him get away with the lie. "You weren't on duty when I got to the beach. Where did you come from?"

Rory didn't answer as they passed beneath an arch into another room, separate from the locker area. And darker. He eased her feet to a tile floor. Before she could look around to discern their new location, Rory steadied her with his left hand and punched something above her head with his right—and holy blessed warm water went streaming down her head, shoulders and back, shocking her chilled skin with blissful heat.

She backed further into what could only be a shower and Rory followed, his grip reassuring on her elbow. "*Ohhhh.*" Her neck loosened, head tipping to one side. "That's perfect. Totally worth almost drowning for."

"Agree to disagree," came his low voice from the other side of the spray. Olive peeked around the stream of water to find Rory battling concern…and something darker. Hotter. His inked chest lifted and fell in a staggered rhythm, steam from the shower dappling him with condensation. "Are you warmed up?"

His gravelly tone of voice turned Olive's nipples to painful points. *I'm wearing a bathing suit. No cover-up. Nothing.* Her arms flew up to cross over her breasts, but that only pushed them up more, so she dropped her hands to their original position. "Did everyone see my boobs?"

"*What?*" His gaze sharpened and snapped to hers. "No. No one saw any part of you they shouldn't." He dragged a hand over his eyes. "But I'm seeing way too damn much right now, Olive. *Are you warmed up?*"

The word yes sprung to her lips, but no sound came out. She was alone in a dark shower with a man who'd stirred something to life inside of her. Something that made her feel…older. Feminine. She'd had crushes on neighborhood boys in the past and swore she'd experienced attraction. Nope. Nothing in her life had come close to the yearning that crawled all over her now, wreaking discomfort and emptiness in places she didn't know such things were possible.

And God. God, it didn't help that Rory was absolutely gorgeous with his wet hair and cords of tan muscles, topped with tattoos so stark, they seemed freshly painted. That wasn't what made her ache, though. No, his eyes did that. They betrayed how aware he was of Olive. That this gravitational force between them was not typical. It wasn't typical at all.

She could no more say the words, "Yes, I'm warmer now," than she could go about the rest of her day without drawing Rory closer. Finding some way to touch him. Be touched. Because if she said those words, they would leave this place. He'd put an end to this thing between them that he'd obviously deemed wrong.

"So…" Operating on their own terms, her fingertips traced the edge of her bikini bottoms. Rory's eyes tracked their progress like a hunter, a violent shudder passing through him. "You're not going to call me. You're just going to be my personal rescue service?"

Restless hands flexed at his sides. "I don't know how to answer that, Olive."

"Try."

A beat passed. His nostrils flared. "I made it through a day without calling you. I was trying to make it through another…and then I saw you in front of someone else's chair, looking like a fuck fantasy that has no place in my head—" He cut himself off with a sharp exhale. "So I switched. I switched so I could be near you. I couldn't help wanting to be near you."

Fuck fantasy. Fuck fantasy. The words pinged around in her head like hailstones off a window. "I picked this bathing suit specifically for its modesty."

"It didn't work."

"Oh." Olive didn't realize she'd stepped back until her shoulder blades pressed to the steam-covered tile wall and she nearly moaned at the sensation of something—anything—touching her skin. The hard surface made her feel provocative. Trapped. She wanted to be trapped between the tile and Rory. "Will you just come here?" she whispered.

A scrape of a sound left his mouth. "I don't know if I can stop touching you once I start. I don't know anything when it comes to you."

The running water sluicing down from above sent wet hair into her face, obscuring her vision, so she pushed it back, let the damp warmth run over her lips. "Please?"

Rory lunged, growling, stopping just short of making contact. His hands slapped the tile above her head, his chest heaving. And then his mouth gave the barest brush of her temple and Olive almost collapsed under the rush of bliss, unable to trap her moan this time.

"Come on, Olive," he said choppily. "Barely touching you and that body reacts like I'm giving it that first hard thrust. You're killing me here."

Trying to think clearly with a new, unfamiliar motor running deep within her body was a challenge, but Olive sensed she had to lure Rory closer. He was still managing to hold himself away from her and she wanted to snap that willpower in half. With a swallow, she settled the palms of her hands against Rory's hard stomach and slid them over the muscular curve of his pectorals. "Thank you for saving me."

His eyelids drooped, his rough exhale sending the shower steam into a swirl. "Don't thank me. Just stop almost dying." He appeared transfixed by her fingers as they splayed over his muscles. "Please?"

"I'll think about it…" Slowly, she went up on her tiptoes and locked her wrists behind his neck. "If you kiss me."

He advanced on her fast, ripping a gasp from her throat when he sandwiched her between his unyielding body and the tile wall. *Oh my God.* Every inch of him was created to correspond with every inch of her. Was that possible? "You think I'm the kind of man you play games with?" His hot puffs of breath fanned her mouth. "You don't know anything about me."

"Tell me. After you kiss me."

His laughter was harsh and lacking all humor. "You don't want me to take what you're offering, Olive. I'll want more. I won't be able to stay away from you." Out of necessity, Olive pushed up and slid their lips together, making his body surge tighter against hers. "This new life of yours is only beginning, and mine…it never got started, all right? Don't torture me," he grated directly against her mouth.

"You're torturing *me*," she said breathily, beginning to grow frustrated with the lack of satisfaction. She needed it so badly without even knowing fully what it entailed. "I can't stop thinking about you."

"*Stop.*" He kissed her. *Hard.* "Stop."

What had been the purpose of Olive's mouth until this moment? As soon as her lips met Rory's, they were given a new reason for existing. Despite his harsh command, there was no stopping once the kiss started. Olive was flattened against the wall, Rory's fingers diving into her hair, weaving the wet strands between them. Olive's arms went limp, dropping from his hair and remaining kind of suspended in a mid-air surrender as Rory's mouth moved over hers, mastering it, ruining her for any other kiss in this lifetime. And then she could only use her hands to pull him close. *Closer. Closer.*

Oh *God*, she couldn't get him to press her into the wall tightly enough. Her body was crying out for something she didn't know how to ask for. Couldn't ask for. Not with his tongue taking blatant, sexual ownership of her mouth. He found her tongue and wound it with his own, the bristle of his beard scraping her chin. Water trickled down between them, making the kiss wetter than it already was.

Olive curled her fingers into the waistband of his red shorts, arching her lower body and pulling Rory closer at the same time. *Give me what I need. What do I need?* At the same time she felt his erection, long and thick against her belly, his mouth let hers go on a guttural groan.

"Tell me what you want." He teased her upper lip with his tongue. "You can't have it unless you say it by name."

"I-I…don't know. I just want to stop aching."

They fell headlong into a moaning kiss. "I want that, too, sunbeam." His right hand left her hair, his palm curving to the side of her neck, traveling lower. Lower. "Can I touch you?"

Their eyes locked and she couldn't look away from his combination of hunger and vulnerability. As if she might say no. Or not trust him. "Yes," she whispered. "Anywhere."

Heat flared in Rory's face, but he hesitated, shaking his head. "God help us both," he muttered, his hands finding her breasts and palming them. Tightly. Like they belonged to him. A line of electricity started at her nipples and rippled to her sex, making Olive's thighs smack together with a loud sound. "There it is," Rory said, cursing. "Been dreaming about those legs snapping together around my hips. Just like that."

Later she might worry about coming across desperate, but in that moment, she could only care about making Rory's words a reality. God. Oh God, she needed pressure against that suffering part of her anatomy. Now. She gripped his shoulders and tried to climb his hard wall of muscle, but he peeled her off with a denial, using his left hand to trap her wrists above her head. A willing prisoner.

"Uh-uh. *No*," he gritted, pressing their foreheads together. "Not unless you want to fuck, Olive. If you sit that ripe, little body on my cock, that's exactly what's going to happen."

The walls of her femininity clenched. *Clenched* at being spoken to—about—in such a way. To be desired this way…to have the proof of her own appeal prodding her in the stomach was a powerful thing. Especially because his appeal was equally vast. The feel of his skin, the intensity of his eyes, the smell of sunscreen and mint and male. A streak of recklessness she'd never encountered spoke on her behalf. "That's what I want. The ache…"

A heavy shudder moved through Rory, and since they were plastered together, it vibrated her body along with his. "You don't mean that," he said thickly, his right hand dropping, slowly cupping her sex and pressing, pressing, grinding his palm against it, drawing a shocked sob from Olive. "You've never had a man anywhere near this, have you?"

"No," she gasped.

"*Fuck*." He pressed his middle finger to her clit, massaging her through the wet material of her bikini bottoms. "Taking this for myself will earn me a place in hell."

"No it won't."

"It's not happening," Rory cut in harshly, quieting her with a hard kiss. "I can take away the ache other ways." Olive's knees weakened as Rory knelt down on the tile floor, the spray rushing over his head as he leaned in, exhaling against the triangle of her bottoms once, twice, before tugging them down to her ankles, devouring the sight of her. "Son of a bitch. It's as beautiful as the rest of you," he rasped, pressing his mouth and nose to her intimate flesh, breathing her in. "Last chance, Olive. Tell me I shouldn't lick your virgin pussy, baby, *please*."

Yeah right. She'd been fantasizing for a long time about having sex, introduced to every aspect of intimacy through books. Even on the page, this kind of foreplay had never really appealed to her. Obviously, she'd been shortsighted since she was practically restraining herself from climbing onto his shoulders. Anything to stop the incessant flames from licking her skin. To stop the churn of frustration inside of her, begging for relief. "Rory." She slipped her fingers into his hair and guided him closer. "I need you."

"You had to say that." He pushed his closed mouth up against her softness, his big shoulders lifting and falling on a groan, then his lips began moving in the open-mouthed writhe of a kiss, the action shifting the flesh shielding her core, easing the sides apart, exposing her clit. His upper lip grazed her nub gently, and Olive almost hit the ceiling. Her reaction seemed to drive Rory a little crazy, his fingertips digging into her hips, yanking her lower body closer to his mouth. The hard, slick glide of his tongue separated her flesh further and journeyed over her clit in a slow, deliberate lick. "Goddamn, you taste so fucking sweet. You going to melt on my tongue like a good girl, Olive?"

"Yes. *Yes.*"

"You make sure to tell me when you're going to come." He razed the inside of her thigh with his teeth, then returned to her private flesh, parting her with another thorough lick. "I want to lap up as much as I can before the shower washes it away."

Olive's head tipped back on its own, her back arching away from the wall. "Oh my God. O-okay. Okay. Oh my God."

Rory formed a V with his fingers, holding her flesh open—and spent a full minute flicking his tongue against her clit without pause or mercy. All the while, Olive babbled begging words, a scream building in her chest, until she finally let it loose.

"*Rory*," she whimpered, growing desperate, the sound of her physical distress still echoing off the walls. "I'm going t-to…"

He took his tongue away but used the pad of his thumb to tease her swollen bundle of nerves, never stopping, never letting up. She watched beneath heavy lids as his licked a path straight up the center of her belly, closing his teeth around the string that connected the triangles of her bikini, nudging them aside. They went easily, since her breasts had essentially heaved themselves halfway to freedom. And the shower pelted his head, coasting down her body as Rory closed his mouth around her nipples, groaning as he sucked them, his fingers masterful between her thighs. "These tits," he growled, licking across to her other breast. "Made me hard clear across the beach."

Olive's stomach shuddered, her vision beginning to blur, tension creeping, coiling in her mid-section. "I hate them," she managed, her legs trembling. "Or I used to? They seem good to go right now—*oh*."

Rory grazed her nipples with his teeth, and a string pulled taut deep inside of her. She begged him in gibberish to do it again, but his mouth was already journeying back downward, replacing his fingers to suckle her clit gently—and Olive saw stars. That gathering pressure beneath her navel gave way like a collapsing cliff and she tasted blood in her mouth, courtesy of attempting to trap her scream of his name. It got loose anyway, bouncing off the walls and sounding nothing like her. She pressed her hips closer to Rory's mouth and writhed on his giving tongue, the orgasm gripping her like an iron fist, squeezing, *squeezing*, her inner walls bearing down, searching for more.

"Inside me," she sobbed, meaning it that moment with every fiber or her being. "Rory, I-I think I need you inside me."

He made a choked noise and stood, pressing their mouths together and they panted for heavy moments, the steam curling around them. "*Shhh.*" His right hand cupped the juncture of her thighs, massaging it gently with his roughened palm. "Easy, sunbeam. Easy. We can't go there." Her thighs tightened around his hand and they groaned into a kiss, the waves of pleasure continuing to coast over her, wracking her with tremors. "Goddammit, I'm not going to survive you," he muttered thickly against her mouth. "I just have to make sure you survive me, okay? Help me do that."

Finally, the shaking lessened and Olive slumped into Rory's welcoming arms. She could feel his long erection between them, trapped by the wet material of his shorts, but every time she tried to reach for it, he caught her wrists and distracted her with kisses…until she was incapable of focusing on anything but the give and take of his tongue, the gruff sounds he made in his throat, the hands that smoothed down her hips, tracing the curve of her waist—

A door crashed open somewhere out in the locker room. Rory tensed and pulled away, visibly struggling to become alert, his breathing labored, pupils dilated. His hands shook as he covered her breasts with the bathing suit top and dragged the bottoms back up her legs. Fighting through her lethargy, Olive reached back and turned off the shower in an attempt to be useful, a veil of silence dropping around them, save their heavy breathing.

"He's too unpredictable," came a weary male voice from the other room. "I can't afford him anymore." A curse. "He's not even answering his phone."

A lightly accented female voice responded. "There has to be an explanation. He's never just left the beach before, has he?"

"No, but it was only a matter of time. We're talking about

the guy who started a bar fight last summer because a customer snapped to get his attention." the male voice answered. "Or the time he just didn't show up at all and called me from a holding cell? I can't make allowances anymore. If someone were to get hurt or worse while his chair is sitting vacant, I could lose the lifeguarding contract with the town."

Olive didn't register that the man was talking about Rory until she noticed the distance in his gaze, the hard line of his jaw. "Stay here," he murmured, backing away from her.

Olive could only watch in silence as Rory sauntered into the locker room, still dripping from their shower. "You can stop calling me, Andrew. I'm right here."

A beat passed. "Where the hell did you go?"

"Had to take care of something." He propped a hand on the archway. "You don't want to make allowances for me anymore, just say the word."

"And you'd be fine with that." Andrew's voice was flat. "Just abandoning ship and leaving me and Jamie to hold everything down?"

"Just trying to give you what you want," Rory shot back, the muscle patterns shifting on his broad back. "Look, I don't get choices, I get marching orders. Would that work for you?"

"You think I do *this* by choice?" There was something written in between the lines of Andrew's incredulity. "We both know I don't."

Olive couldn't resist a step forward to peek at the newcomers. She'd barely managed to see around Rory's elbow when she locked eyes with the woman. A *gorgeous* young woman with an apron tied around her waist, her long, dark hair in a braid. Her eyes widened when she saw Olive, but instead of drawing attention to her presence in the shower, the woman snagged a towel from a stack near the lockers and oh-so-casually sidestepped in Olive's direction, holding it out. Olive took the offering with a whispered thank you, deciding they were going to be friends.

They didn't get away with their covert mission, however.

"Is someone *in* there with you?" Andrew asked.

Rory blocked her more completely. "That's my business."

"For fuck's sake, Rory."

It had taken Olive a minute to regain her wits and process the conversation. Now that she'd come back down to earth, the reality of the situation was hitting home. Rory was in trouble for leaving the beach with her. Was he getting fired? She couldn't let him lose his job because she'd kept him from it. The guilt would kill her. Not to mention, he was incredible at being a lifeguard. Hadn't he just proven that? Who did this guy Andrew think he was?

Olive wrapped the towel around her shoulders and marched out of the shower. "Excuse me." She lost a little steam at the sight of Andrew, who was easily the second-hottest man she'd ever witnessed up close, right behind Rory—Rory, who tried to block her from view. Olive dodged him. "This man just saved my life. He was *heroic*," she sputtered. "I would have drowned if he hadn't reached me in time. It's my fault he left the beach. I was freezing to death and…pretty scared, okay? If you're going to blame someone, blame me."

Andrew crossed his arms over his chest and regarded her with curiosity. "You are aware that rescuing someone doesn't involve a complimentary shower, right?"

"Don't," Rory said quietly, his hands flexing in a dangerous way that Olive now recognized. "Do *not* question her, Andrew. I'm warning you."

Oddly, Rory's threat seemed to drain some of Andrew's irritation. He split a look between Rory and Olive, a groove forming between his eyebrows.

"Why don't you men talk about this at home?" The woman gave Andrew a pointed look. "When we've all calmed down a little." When no one said anything, she rolled her eyes and approached Olive with a hand extended. "I'm Jiya. I had the misfortune of moving in next door to these stubborn Irish mules."

Olive couldn't help her smile as they shook. "Oh..." She glanced up at Rory to find his expression shuttered. "Are you brothers?"

He gave a tight nod. "This is Andrew."

"And you are..." his brother prompted.

"Olive." She rolled her lips together in the following silence. "I should head home so Rory can get back to work."

Andrew nodded curtly. "I've only got his chair covered for the next half hour."

"Perfect. That's enough time to get her home alive." Rory bent to one side and picked up her beach bag, which she had no recollection of retrieving from the beach. When she saw her glasses and the Freud towel stuffed inside, she almost kissed Rory full on the mouth. Until he said, "She has a habit of tempting death."

Her sniff of protest hung in the air as Rory threaded their fingers together and pulled her toward his locker. He set down the beach bag on the bench and replaced the glasses on her nose with a look of concentration. With a few twists of his wrists, he sprung the metal teeth of his locker, reached inside and took out a gray T-shirt, dropping it over her head. But not before a piece of white paper fluttered to the ground between them. It was the straw wrapper with her number on it.

Forgetting all about their audience, Olive beamed up at Rory as he pulled her hands through the arm holes of the massive shirt. With her heart in her throat, she watched him stoop down to pick up the straw wrapper and place it carefully back on the shelf, like it was a priceless artifact. Then, seeming to realize how telling the action was, he slapped the locker shut and guided her toward the exit. "I, uh…forget that was in there."

"Rory?"

"What, sunbeam?"

"I don't believe you."

CHAPTER SIX

Rory was going to drop Olive off and get the hell away. That's what he should have done after pulling her out of the water. Wrapped her in a towel and radioed one of the female lifeguards to bring her somewhere warm. Or called one of her friends to come pick her up. He never should have brought her into the Hut—into their own private world where none of the consequences of touching her existed. Where the weight of his past and the shine of her future were blurred by the steam.

Even now, knowing he shouldn't, Rory couldn't keep himself from holding her hand. It made him feel like a fucking giant walking down the street, having this girl beside him. And yet it was impossible to miss the way passersby looked at them. Since he'd given Olive his only spare shirt, he was bare chested, his tattoos busier than the intersection they were crossing. Some of the people they passed knew Rory from the neighborhood and averted their eyes, giving him wide berth on the sidewalk. Did Olive notice?

He hoped she did. Hoped she realized the local hothead had no business with a pretty blonde angel in thick-rimmed glasses and college courses lined up. He needed to scare her away once and for all, because this crazy connection between them was like an overloaded circuit breaker, capable of setting his world on fire. He'd been worried that spending time with Olive would amount to him feeling…possessive. Or worse, optimistic that something lasting could come out of it. He'd done *a lot* more than spend time with her, though. And something had happened in the dark of the shower that felt irreversible. They'd communicated things with their bodies he didn't know how to say out loud.

Mine.

No. She *wasn't* his. Tell that to the organ in his chest that wouldn't stop racing, though. Tell that to his primed body. His mind, which refused to stop reminding Rory that she screamed when he teased her clit long enough. That she kissed him like she didn't give a shit about oxygen. Christ, she was incredible.

"Is Andrew your only brother?"

"No." He cleared his throat. "No, there are three of us. Andrew is the oldest, which is why he acts like the king prick sometimes. Not sure if you noticed." They shared a wry smile. "Jamie is in the middle. Then me."

"Are you all lifeguards?"

"Yeah. Every summer since we were sixteen." Discomfort crept up the back of his neck. "Although I missed a couple of summers a while back." When Olive looked at him, obviously waiting for an explanation, he changed the direction of the conversation, needing to live in this world a little longer. A world where she didn't know the extent of his depravity. "Jamie teaches during the school year. Economics. He's smart like you."

Olive opened her mouth and closed it again. "Um, thank you." She paused. "Don't tell him, but I hate economics. It's too cut and dried. Not enough room for theories or gray areas."

"I'm telling him."

"Don't." She poked Rory in the side with her free hand and the move was so cute, he almost stopped walking to kiss her. Just wanted to yank her up on her toes and work her innocent body into another frenzy, like he'd done in the shower. But he kept walking, jaw clenched. As if sensing Rory trying to create distance between them, she launched into a ramble. "I mean, I guess there is *something* to be said for gray areas. Right? That's where light and dark come together. If they always stayed separate, life would be pretty boring."

Was she talking about them? Trying to convince him he had a right to walk beside her on the street? To *be* with her? He wouldn't allow himself to be convinced. Rory looked ahead and realized they were entering the more expensive area where the rents ticked up by a couple grand. "How much farther?" he asked without making eye contact.

"A couple of blocks."

Her subdued tone filled him with concern. "You feeling okay? Cold again?"

"I'm fine." She regarded him thoughtfully. "I was just thinking about what you said, back in the locker room. When you were talking to your brother."

Rory exhaled hard, trying and failing not to think of Andrew's disappointed expression. Shouldn't he be used to it by now? "Which part?"

Olive seemed hesitant, watching him through her lashes. "That you don't get choices. You get marching orders. What did you mean?"

"That I don't get trusted with a lot of responsibility. Andrew tells us where to go. When to be there." He tried to sound less frustrated but couldn't pull it off. "Jamie has other shit going on, though. Teaching, his books. I just get a schedule and a lot of skepticism that I can stick to it."

"Do you earn that skepticism?"

"Yeah. I do." He raked a hand through his hair. "What's the point of being efficient if I'll never go any higher than where I'm at, you know? This is it. I'm a name on a schedule."

She seemed genuinely confused. "Is that all you want to be?"

"No." Rory heard the word come out of his mouth before his brain registered it. *Did* he want more than lifeguarding and pouring drinks? Was an ex-con wanting more out of the daily grind just wishful thinking? When he started to consider the answer might be no...or at the very least a gray area, hope trickled in—and it alarmed him. He'd been so devoid of hope or light at the end of the tunnel, he didn't know how to handle it. What if he tried and found out for certain that there had never been a point? For damn sure, nothing he did would be good enough to deserve the girl walking beside him with such trust.

Olive blinked up at Rory and he realized he was staring. "Andrew also said...he said you called him from a holding cell once?"

His stomach took a dive toward the sidewalk. Had part of him wished she'd missed that part of Andrew and Jiya's conversation? Why? It would be counterproductive when his goal was to bring this girl to her expensive apartment building and split. To leave her alone for good.

That's why he had her hand locked in a death grip, right?

Rory pulled Olive to a stop on the sidewalk and forced himself to untangle their fingers, pushing them through his hair instead. "I should have been more upfront with you, Olive, okay?" He tried to swallow, but his mouth was too dry. "When I thought we'd never make it past those milkshakes, I thought I'd get away with not telling you. So you wouldn't look back and think of me as...that ex-con you almost accidentally dated. I didn't want that. But here we are. And I still have your phone number even though I damn well shouldn't. So you need to know, sunbeam, that I'm not lying when I say I'm not a good guy. I'm not good for you."

The breeze blew the blonde hair around her face. "So you were…"

"The night I called Andrew was a separate occasion. But yeah, Olive. I've done time in prison." *Just do it. Cut this off before you fall any deeper for this girl.* She would wise up someday down the road, when it was too late, and he'd have to sever an arm to let her go. He'd be her villain. "I put a guy in a coma. With my fists. That's the kind of man who you just defended back there as heroic. That was real sweet and all, baby, but it's not true."

He heard her swallow over the rush of traffic on the avenue. "What happened?"

"It doesn't matter. Nothing excuses it, Olive," he said adamantly. "Or the fact that I'm still not great at controlling my temper. You feel it. You *know*. I've gone looking for fights since I was a kid—it's a nice, little trait I inherited from my father. Men fight. Men swing their fists and ask questions later. That's what I do."

Her expression told Rory the times he'd almost lost his cool with the waiter and Andrew hadn't gone unnoticed. "How long were you away?"

"How long was I *in prison*? That's where I went." He ground his molars together, hating this after period they'd entered. *After she found out.* He'd lay odds on her searching for a break in the conversation so she could sprint for safety. "A little under two years, starting when I was eighteen. On an assault change."

A degree of color left her face. "The man is okay?"

"Yeah, he's fine now. Jamie checked. But we don't exactly exchange Christmas cards."

Even with the passing traffic and the ocean roar in the distance, the silence that dropped over them was deafening. "Okay, I get it, Rory. You're not ideal boyfriend material." He didn't breathe as seconds ticked past. "Is that what you're trying to tell me?"

"Yeah," he said hoarsely. "You have to go. You have to get away."

Olive flinched but kept her chin up. "So, fine. I'm going to walk away now. And you're going to let me go, right? You're going to throw away my number and I'll eventually forget who gave me this T-shirt. Fine with me."

Direct hit. Was there an arrow sticking out of his chest? "It's not *fine* with me. I never said it was fine," he managed. "I'm just doing the right thing by you."

"By dropping me? I kind of left Oklahoma to get away from people doing that to me, so it's a good thing I found out early that this can't go anywhere." The light sheen in her eyes made his chest ache. "I'm meeting Leanne in the morning to study. We have a test early Monday morning and…I have to go. Bye, Rory."

When she breezed past him, Rory swore she ripped off a layer of skin. His stomach shot up into his mouth as Olive moved farther away down the sidewalk, the sound of her sandals fading and blending into the traffic. Jesus, he was going to be sick. He started to go after her, already counting the seconds until he could get his arms around her, but he froze in his tracks when Olive stopped in front of the nicest building on the block. A uniformed man opened the door for her—and the dude must have seen them together, because he sent a look of distaste across the street.

Olive paused in the entrance, turning back toward Rory and all but imploring him to come and get her. But he hesitated. That doorman had the right idea. He didn't belong within ten feet of a girl like Olive. Her college career was on the horizon and she was set up, living in the best building money could afford. So although it killed him, he took off down the sidewalk, glancing back a moment later to find her gone. Out of sight.

Feeling like he'd been hit by a truck, Rory leaned back against the closest building. She'd compared him to the family that had essentially abandoned her. Couldn't she see this wasn't to serve his own self-interest? If he allowed himself to be selfish, they would spend every available second together. He would ride her to classes on his bike. He'd watch over her on the beach and buy her so many milkshakes, she'd get sick of them.

No. No, she'd walked away, too, right? He'd told her everything and she'd made the decision that was right for her. She hadn't argued or tried to make light of what he'd done in the past—because it wasn't possible. There was no light angle, it was all dark. He'd done the right thing here. Olive was too young, her future too promising, to get caught up with an older man with so little to offer and a reputation for fighting to boot.

Go. Turn and go.

His feet might as well have been encased in concrete boots, but Rory managed to walk back to the beach, emptiness spreading a little further to the corners of his stomach with every single step.

RORY SAT ON the top step of the house the next morning, watching oranges and reds thread their fingers into the sky. He'd slept approximately eighteen minutes the night before, so he couldn't exactly appreciate the beauty of nature. He could only think about Olive having an early study date with her friend. How was she getting there? The bus? Did she have a car he didn't know about?

What if something bad happened and he wasn't there to save her?

He tossed the dregs of his freezing cold coffee into the bushes, set the mug down and scrubbed his hands down his face. She'd called his bluff. No sense in denying it. He'd been awake enough hours and replayed their conversation in his head so many times, he could recite it word for word. Yeah, he'd meant what he said to Olive. There couldn't be a relationship between them. They lived in different worlds. They were going different places.

But he hadn't really allowed himself to consider what it would be like *never* talking to her again. Never seeing or kissing her again. A world where none of those things were possible left him lifeless, staring out into the sunrise trying to remember if there was a point to going through the motions every day, like he'd been doing for so long.

Since returning home from prison, he hadn't allowed himself to be ambitious. Wasn't ambition kind of pointless with a prison record? How far could a man reasonably go with an assault attached to his name? Even without a record, his hair trigger energy made people uneasy. On the nights he bartended at the Castle Gate, conversations were kept to a quieter pitch. Customers chose to sit at tables instead of in front of him at the bar. Every once in a while, a woman would be attracted to the very same energy that made others wary, but until Olive, Rory hadn't realized how uncomfortable those women made him. They looked at him and saw a novelty. A one-time thrill.

No one had ever looked at him the way Olive did. No judgment. Only curiosity, awareness…and that complicated something between them that he didn't have a name for. Like she wanted to explore him. Like she couldn't help wanting to. Needing to.

What would it be like to have Olive look up at him with such trust and open admiration…and know he'd *earned* it? To be a good man for her?

Pointless thoughts. Rory traced some carvings on the concrete stairs with the toe of his sneakers. His initials, along with Andrew's and Jamie's. He could still remember the afternoon they'd used a stick to alter the wet cement. How their father had reacted when he got home that night from running the Castle Gate. Their mother had borne the brunt of his anger. She always had—and they'd been too young to do anything about it.

Back then, anyway.

As always, when Rory thought of that time, the nape of his neck turned hot, wire seeming to stretch his fingers, curl them into fists. When he'd gotten sentenced, his mother and father had still been living together in the house. Jamie had been a senior in college, on the brink of earning his degree in Education, Andrew was beginning to take over the family business and working constantly. That left eighteen-year-old Rory alone with his parents in the house. By then, he'd grown taller and broader than his father. It went unspoken that he would protect his mother and win.

Until the night on the beach when he'd given in to his anger.

Hard to protect anyone from inside of a cell.

The door of the house opened, saving Rory from his darkening thoughts. When both of his brothers emerged barefoot in sweatpants and hoodies, Rory ignored them, continuing to stare out at the horizon in stony silence.

Jamie sat on the bottom step. Andrew took the one beside him. No one said anything, except for the neighborhood, which spoke its own language of cars rumbling to life, seagulls calling to each other on the breeze, the Atlantic Ocean waking up in the distance.

Finally, Andrew broke the silence. "I'm sorry about what I

said yesterday. About not being able to afford you. Especially after you'd just been through a rescue. A tough one." He scratched at his morning beard. "I was just pissed off."

Rory waved a dismissive hand, even though a shift took place in his chest. "It's fine, man."

"No, it's not." Andrew shifted on the step. "Look. This girl Olive is obviously important to you and she overheard—"

"I said it's fine." Hearing her name out loud cracked him straight down the middle, so it took him a few seconds to continue. "My brother bitching about me and saying I'm unpredictable wasn't the deal breaker."

Jamie turned to face them with a curious expression. "You told her about prison?"

His jaw clenched "Had to be done."

"I assume you told her how it happened." Jamie prompted. "*Why* it happened."

"It doesn't make a difference, Jamie."

"Sorry, but fuck that. It makes a difference to me."

A stone lodged itself in Rory's throat. "I didn't mean to imply it wasn't important. Only that the outcome is the same, no matter what prompted me to almost kill a man."

No one spoke for a moment, all of them probably recalling the day he'd been cuffed and thrown into the back of a police car. The guilty plea that followed, despite being advised otherwise by his court-appointed attorney. He'd done the crime, hadn't he? So he'd pay for it.

"So *was* it a deal breaker?" Andrew asked, easing the building tension with a half-smile. "Because she came to your defense pretty hard in the Hut. If she'd had a bat handy, I'd be limping behind the bar tonight."

Half of Rory wanted them to stop talking about Olive. The

other half? Didn't want to talk about anything *but* her. The latter half won by a landslide. "I'm not sure it broke the deal. I think I might have crushed it before she got the chance."

Jamie's sigh was long suffering. "I didn't even get the opportunity to judge her."

"You'd have loved her," Rory said, pressing his thumbs into his eye sockets to try and stop the images of her walking away over and over again. "She almost got hit by a fucking bus because a book distracted her."

"Which book?"

"I think I've seen you read it before. Something by Vonnegut."

"How dare you mess this up for me," Jamie deadpanned. "I kind of hate you."

He laughed, but it lacked authenticity. "Join the club."

The three of them watched as a group of joggers ran past down in the middle of the street, moving in the direction of the boardwalk. Not an unusual sight in Long Beach, but groups of joggers that size didn't usually route themselves through a residential area—especially one on the lower end of the income spectrum.

"You ever seen them pass through this way before?"

"No," Andrew responded with a head shake. "And I'm always up at this time working."

Jamie and Rory traded an eye roll.

But when they eased back into silence, Rory couldn't stop thinking about the joggers. They got up every morning, same as him. Odds are, most of them didn't love their jobs. They were probably tired, needed vacations. But despite all of it, they woke up every morning and achieved a goal. They took different routes to reach it, changed, adapted to the terrain and worked toward something that satisfied them.

All right, so maybe the joggers weren't the *first* to shake these new revelations loose. He'd spent a lot of time staring up at the ceiling last night. Thinking of Olive, yeah, but he'd also done a lot of wondering about himself. How long could he expect to continue in this same repetitive holding pattern of lifeguarding and bartending with nothing to show for it? He was already tired of it at twenty-four. He never reached a goal, like the joggers did.

Hell, like his brothers did. Little by little, Andrew improved the Castle Gate, turning it from a dive to a respected neighborhood staple. No longer the kid who'd one day inherit the landmark bar, he was now a legitimate businessman. Jamie would receive his teaching tenure soon. Sometimes Rory thought their middle brother fell back into their patented routine of lifeguarding and bartending every summer because it was a family custom. Really, though, with his intelligence and college degree, he could do *anything*.

That left Rory. He *couldn't* do anything he wanted.

But maybe it was time to try *something*.

To set a goal and jog for it.

Rory cleared his throat. "I know it's not the best time to ask, seeing as how I fucked up yesterday, but, uh…" Striving for casual even though his pulse was ticking his ears, Rory shrugged. "You're stressed out, A. Between the bar and the beach, you've got at least sixty employees to juggle." No matter how hard he tried, he couldn't make eye contact with Andrew, afraid he'd see wariness there. "I've been around long enough to know how to place liquor orders for the bar. Receive deliveries. Make sure the kitchen and bar are stocked. You can show me how to do payroll." He swallowed. "Let me help."

Rory stared out at the horizon and held his breath, waiting

for a response. He could feel Jamie trading a silent look with their older brother, probably shocked out of their minds. That made three of them. As he waited for the verdict that suddenly seemed like the most important one of his life, thoughts of Olive crept in. Chances were slim to none that he'd ever be a college graduate. Or someone who read a ton of books. Odds were he'd never have a nine-to-five.

Still. He couldn't help but wonder... If he changed his route and worked hard enough, could Olive be proud to be with a guy like him?

"Can you get to the bar early tonight?" Andrew asked, squinting one eye over at him. "Payroll is a little tricky, but it shouldn't take you long to pick it up."

"Yeah," Rory said thickly, relief filtering in, warming him with something that resembled hope. "I can do that."

Several heavy beats passed before Jamie put a hand over his heart and spoke. "Here we are, trapped in the amber of the moment—"

"Christ," Rory muttered, coming to his feet and turning before Jamie could see his smile. "Shut up, Jamie."

His middle brother stood, too. "Don't interrupt me when I'm quoting Vonnegut."

Jiya chose that moment to arrive at the bottom of the stoop, an apron dangling from her hand. "What did I miss?"

"Nothing," all three brothers said at the same time.

It didn't feel like nothing, though. It felt like the beginning of *something*.

CHAPTER SEVEN

OLIVE SAT IN the window of a coffee shop sipping an iced coffee and skipping around between her favorite scenes of *Hitchhiker's Guide to the Galaxy*, her go-to comfort read. Every person who passed by the glass storefront were jovial, relaxed. On their way to the beach. She wanted to follow in their wake and warm herself in the sunshine again, but she remained glued to the chair, shivering in the air conditioning. She reached the part in the book where the reader meets Zaphod Beeblebrox, a two-headed, three-armed former president of the Galaxy—and ship thief—dismayed when she didn't experience her usual sense of solace.

She hadn't been back to the beach in two weeks. Two weeks since she'd been pulled from the ocean, had a sexual awakening and been cast aside. All in a matter of hours. It was impressive, really, how many peaks and valleys she'd managed to cram into one afternoon. Maybe she should call Guinness and apply for world record status.

Olive grimaced into a sip of watered-down coffee. It wasn't like her to be so negative, but she'd taken a lot longer to recover from Rory Prince than expected. As in, she hadn't recovered. Hardly at all. Every time she left her apartment, she swore he would be waiting outside, that serious, *this-is-a-bad-idea* expression cemented on his gorgeous face. Walking through Long Beach, she always had the fresh sense she'd just missed seeing him. Which was crazy. *She* was crazy.

Her focus should be squarely on acing her summer class and beginning a sterling college career. And it had. She'd been more meticulous than usual when writing papers and studying for quizzes, mostly in the name of distraction. She only allowed herself to pine for Rory after she finished her homework, and she almost always stuck to that incentive/reward system.

Just kidding.

This cavernous feeling in her stomach refused to be filled, no matter how many food truck dinners she fed it. It would, though. It had to, because Rory obviously wasn't coming back. Nor was he going to call the number she'd scrawled on the straw wrapper. Was it still in his locker?

For the millionth time in the last two weeks, she wondered if she'd walked away from Rory too soon. He'd just told her something serious. A *majorly* serious thing. That he'd been in prison for putting a man in a coma. A smart girl such as herself was well within the parameters of common sense to run away and never look back. Except for two things.

One, he'd practically tripped over himself to make sure Olive knew he was bad news. Would someone with a conscience do that? Or would they act selfishly, take what they wanted and let the other person suffer in due course?

And the second reason she should have checked herself before turning away?

The way he made her feel wasn't going to come around again. At only eighteen years old, people might laugh at her for being so *positive* of that notion. Well, so be it. She absorbed a little more knowledge with every book she read. Olive had walked in a million sets of shoes, throughout dozens of unique genres, living through the heartache of others and combing through the world's philosophies while hidden away on the second floor of her parents' house. She'd only lived for eighteen years, but her soul held the weight of lifetimes. If she never saw Rory again, she would wonder what they could have been until she grew old. She just *knew* it. That's why she'd shouted at him to come back the day they'd met. It's why she couldn't sleep anymore.

And God, wasn't that terrifying? All of it. It was so scary, she didn't think the air conditioner was responsible for making her shiver anymore.

Rory, this person she'd felt drawn to so entirely since laying eyes on him…had blown her off. Two weeks later, there was no denying that. The day they'd broken up—because a break-up is exactly how it had felt, even if they weren't boyfriend and girlfriend—she'd compared Rory to her parents. It had been an emotional response and she'd regretted throwing it in his face.

Now, though? She wasn't so sure she wanted Rory to show up again.

One afternoon at age fourteen, after finishing her schoolwork early, she'd gone out to see a movie. When it didn't hold her interest, she'd left the theater early and come home to find her parents shooting a video with her siblings. They'd turned to find her in the hallway, guilt written all over their faces. Her brother and sister had been covered in finger paint, laughter frozen on their faces. They'd deliberately left her out of a filming session. And that had been the beginning of the family division; Olive on one side, everyone else on the other. She'd tiptoed through her own house so as not to disrupt their progress, chest panging over the distant sounds of giggling, the pride and encouragement in her parents' voices. Sure, her mother and father had made an effort to engage her after the videos had been filmed, edited and uploaded to YouTube, but those conversations never stopped seeming forced.

If they'd left her out of the videos at a younger age, Olive probably would have been relieved. But by age fourteen, they'd been entertaining the masses for years and she'd already become known among people in town as *that internet girl*. They'd seen her sleeping, brushing her teeth, crying, getting haircuts and having her tonsils removed. To suddenly have that identity taken away after working so hard to live within it…was hard. *Really* hard.

It seemed as though abandonment came in more than one form. Rory dropping her like a bad habit wasn't on par with her parents losing interest in her. But it left Olive with the same hollowness and uncertainty. She and Rory had only known each other for *three days* when he'd left her reeling. What would a relationship with him be like? Constantly waiting and worrying for the next time his conscience flared up? She should be grateful he'd ended it sooner rather than later.

Olive was rubbing at the ever-present tightness in her throat when her cell phone rang in her pocket. Just like every other time it had rung for the last two weeks, her heart shot up into her mouth. It wasn't him, though. Thank God.

Right?

"Hey, Leanne," she answered, twisting the straw of her drink. A line formed between her eyes when laughing male voices could be heard on the other end. "What's up?"

"We're going out tonight," Leanne squealed back. "You know that sophomore in our Intro to Psych class? I ran into her while getting takeout tacos and she invited me to hang out—she has a place off campus—and all these freaking *senior guys* are here. *Athletes*, Olive."

"What kind?"

"The athletic kind."

Olive giggled into the back of her wrist. "Continue."

"They invited us out tonight. We're going out. To *bars*."

"We are?"

"*Yes*. I'm playing the buddy system card."

She'd only known Leanne since the first day of class, but they'd bonded over a love of Pavlov and made each other laugh. It had been a while since Olive had clicked with another girl who hadn't known her as a YouTube personality *first* and Olive second. It was refreshing and comfortable and Olive didn't want Leanne going out with near-strangers alone, whether they went to Stony Brook or not. Especially since they were both lacking in the adult party experience department. Just the idea of dressing up and making small talk exhausted her, though. Not to mention, going out with boys…just the idea of it made her feel unfaithful to Rory. Which was ridiculous. And *stupid*.

Nonetheless, Olive's knee jiggled under the window bar as she tried to come up with an excuse to *not* go. She was disappointing herself, but so be it. Two weeks hadn't been long enough to get the green-eyed lifeguard out of her head and—

A motorcycle rumbled to a stop at the light, across the street from the coffee shop. The rider's fingers stretched on the handlebars in a way she recognized, along with the tense shoulders, the rangy build. No, it couldn't be him. Could it?

He took off the helmet and shoved a hand through his hair, making some adjustment to the face shield before replacing the protective gear on his head.

Olive almost dropped the phone. It *was* him.

Without realizing it, she'd slid off her stool and hidden her body partially behind a pillar. The hair on her skin stood straight up, her pulse in a permanent spike. How dare he look even more gorgeous and masculine than she remembered? She'd never seen him on the bike before and something about the scene excited Olive despite her best efforts. Her palms started to sweat and she dragged her free one down the leg of her shorts, his voice drifting into her head from out of nowhere.

Been dreaming about those legs snapping together around my hips. Just like that.

What would it be like to ride behind him on that bike?

"Olive?"

Leanne's prompt brought her back to the present. "Oh I'm, yeah. I'm here."

As if he'd heard her voice, Rory's head whipped in direction, but Olive drew back behind the pillar just in time, attempting to draw in a calming measure of oxygen through her nose.

"What is going on?" Leanne asked. "Are you okay?"

I don't know.

But as the engine of Rory's motorcycle revved, the purr moving farther and farther into the distance, Olive got good and irritated. *Look at me.* Hiding from a guy. Avoiding the beach. Crying at Allstate commercials. Rory Prince should be changing his routine to avoid *her*. She'd opened herself up to him and he'd rejected the offering. That didn't mean she should mope around and forget why she moved to Long Beach. This was the summer she embraced new beginnings and prepared to start her college career. Leanne and her other classmates were living their lives and there was no reason she shouldn't do the same.

"Leanne," Olive said, her spine snapped straight. "What time are we going out tonight?"

Wow. Underage drinking wasn't even a challenge. Were the police aware of this?

A senior lacrosse player named Zed passed Olive a foaming second beer in as many bars and she thanked him, saluting as he watched and taking a small sip. He put up his arms in exaggerated victory and she made herself laugh through the bitter taste.

Leanne nudged her in the ribs as Zed joined a rowdy conversation with the four other senior guys and girls along for the night. "He likes you."

"Oh, yeah?" Olive assessed Zed, powerless to do anything but compare his Captain America good looks to Rory's villainous ones—and annoyingly preferring the latter. "Cool. Want to share this beer with me?"

"That's all you have to say?" Leanne rolled her eyes and took the beer, drinking deeply. "God, that's gross."

"I know. I wish he'd stop buying them for me."

"Because you're not interested in him? Or the beer?"

Both. Instead of voicing that opinion out loud, however, she forced herself to remember her resolve from earlier that day. She had to stop looking for Rory Prince around every corner and start *enjoying* herself. Zed was a decent sort, if a little boisterous. They'd started on one end of West Beech Street, grabbing food truck empanadas and piling into KJ's Saloon. After that, they'd taken their beer buzz to the boardwalk, Olive and Leanne hanging back and watching the guys' antics. Zed had started a bench hopping competition between the guys that had earned them exasperated looks from passersby. Olive could relate, finding Zed a tad on the immature side. Although, maybe she wasn't in the best frame of mind for exploring new horizons and she should reserve judgment.

Leanne leaned in and tapped her arm. "You're thinking about the guy from the milkshake shop, aren't you?" Olive's surprise turned Leanne's features smug. "The guy who asked for your *numbah.*"

She started to deny the claim but gave in almost immediately. "How do you know? I purposely haven't said a word about him."

"Are you forgetting we're psych majors? Not mentioning him was the dead giveaway."

"Bravo." Olive nodded, impressed. "You might as well skip right to graduation."

Leanne considered. "But then I'd miss gross beer and dick jokes."

"You're not into these dudes, either, are you?"

"God no. And I had such high hopes." She sighed. "Thanks a lot, Hollywood."

They laughed so loud the group of seniors sent them suspicious looks. "Do we just leave? What is the protocol here?"

Two hands slapped down on their table. "Drink up, ladies. We're heading to the next place." Leanne handed Zed the beer and they watched as he made quick work of the remaining golden liquid, before plunking it onto the table. "Are you not entertained, freshman?"

Olive tried not to groan as they followed the noisy group from the bar. She and Leanne walked arm in arm on the boardwalk, pointing out places they wanted to try next time—preferably alone. The guys resumed their bench hopping competition and even though they were twice as drunk and ungainly this time, Olive decided she was having a good time. So two nerds hadn't meshed well with some senior jocks. So what? It wasn't exactly surprising.

Plus, the awkwardness of the night had allowed her to bond with Leanne. Having been homeschooled, Olive hadn't grown up with a lot of close friends. Mostly just acquaintances from the neighborhood and church. Her mutual interests with Leanne made it easy to open up, though, and as they walked and Leanne shared details about her upbringing, Olive found herself doing the same, even confiding how YouTube had divided her family. Olive knew talking about it would help. Hello psychology. She just wondered when the memories would loosen their grip on the present. Tonight was about relaxing. A new start. So she set aside the past and tried to enjoy.

The wind blew in off the Atlantic and Olive closed her eyes as it rushed over her bare shoulders and legs, lifting the fall of blonde hair off her neck. A new calm encompassed her in a wave as they waded through a crowd of outdoor smokers into a new bar—and that's where her calm shattered into a thousand pieces. Because there was Rory behind the bar, pulling a pint of beer from a white-handled tap. Just like earlier when she'd seen him through the coffee shop window, his head turned in her direction like she'd called his name.

They locked eyes and she sucked in a breath, no way to brace for the impact of having the man's attention on her again. But it didn't take any time at all for that attention to drift to Zed who'd thrown an arm around her shoulders to guide her through the crowd…

CHAPTER EIGHT

ONE SECOND HE'D been in the zone. The rhythm bartenders fall into on a busy night like tonight. Pour drink, take cash, ring it up, drop off the change, move on to the next customer. All while clearing empty glasses, getting them washed and ready to use again. Fast, fast, fast. No time to notice anything but the immediate mob of thirsty patrons crowding the bar. On top of his usual bartending routine, he noticed new things now.

Over the last couple of weeks, ordering supplies had been on Rory's shoulders, so he noticed when the foam heads on his Sam Adams pours started to get smaller and made a notation to order another keg tomorrow from the supplier. The ice machine had started to hum louder, so he scheduled the repair man. He sent the staff on their breaks and took phone calls for larger groups that wanted reserved seating. Having more weight on his shoulders was nice. Not only did it seem to motivate him, increase his focus…these new things helped distract him from the utter fucking agony of not being with Olive Cunningham for fourteen days.

Nothing looked the same anymore. The world had changed now that he knew she lived inside of it, the knowledge of her existence carved into every cell of his being.

And so he felt Olive the moment she crossed the threshold of the Castle Gate. Felt a twist in his gut, causing his rhythm to hitch.

Jesus. Christ.

She looked incredible, all drowsy smiles and a silk tank top tucked into her white mini skirt. Her glasses sat perched on her nose, making her adorable on top of sexy. Every man repositioned themselves to watch her enter. As if that didn't wreak immediate havoc on his sanity, some guy put an arm around her—and Rory saw fucking stars. Bright, blinding, sharp-cornered pings of torture in his direct vision, as if his brain was trying to block out the offensive sight in the name of self-preservation.

Beer coasted down over his knuckles and he dropped the glass onto the copper drain with a loud rattle that was immediately absorbed by the pumping music. People waved money in his face and shouted drink orders, but he couldn't hear any of it. He could only watch in horror as some sweaty, Ralph Lauren polo shirt-wearing asshole leaned down and said something way too close to Olive's face.

Rory growled, his right hand gripping the bar so tight, the wood grains made impressions on his palm. Was that her boyfriend? Did she have *a boyfriend*?

"Hey." Jamie came up beside Rory and handed him a towel. "You all right?"

Olive's face came into view again as she passed through the crowd and Rory made a choked sound, barely stopping himself from vaulting over the bar to drag her away from another man. He couldn't even describe how she was looking at him? Half-indignant, half…apologetic? Rory didn't like it. Was he just supposed to stand there and watch someone paw her? Jesus, he couldn't do it. He'd lose his mind.

"That's Olive, isn't it?" Jamie muttered. "Fuck, man."

"I have to go get her…" Rory muttered, lunging for the hatch that would let him out from behind the bar. Jamie blocked him, however, before he could reach it. Anyone else would have regretted that move, but Rory would rather lose his limbs than lay a finger on his middle brother, and Jamie knew it. "Get out of the way. He's *touching* her."

"Listen to me, Rory. She's not your property." Jamie laid his hands on Rory's shoulders. "You're not even dating her."

Yet every second that passed was strangling him, making it harder and harder to breathe. "Olive…she's…I'm not good enough for her," he managed. "Neither is anyone else. Neither is that guy."

"Not your call."

"*Move, Jamie.*"

"Uh-uh."

There was a shout from somewhere deep in the crowded bar. And Rory's world started to move in slow motion. The customers closest to the bar turned to face the commotion and there was a break in the mass of bodies. The guy who'd had his arm around Olive was now facing off with a Castle Gate regular Rory recognized. Polo Shirt shoved the regular and shouted something Rory couldn't hear over the music, but it made the regular shove him back. And then the fists started flying.

"Olive," Rory breathed, rattling the shelves of bottles as he dodged Jamie, attempting to reach her before one of those fists came within two feet of her. Before he could lift the hatch, though, he could only watch in horror as Polo Shirt swung on the regular, got blocked and stumbled backwards, running into Olive hard and sending her stumbling. She went down, knocking her head on the side of a table as she went—and a bomb detonated inside Rory.

He was only vaguely aware that his angry bellow brought the

bar—and the fight—to a standstill, because he could only see her. The way she grimaced and pressed a hand to her head. *Hurt. She's hurt.*

This time, he didn't bother using the fucking hatch. He launched himself over the bar, upsetting bottles and spilling drinks, red bleeding into the edges of his vision. People darted out of his way as he stalked toward the man who'd knocked Olive over. His fists were two rocks, shaking at his sides, lifting, ready to do some serious damage and God, it was going to feel so good. He might have cleaned this fucker's clock just for walking in with Olive. For thinking he could breathe the same air as her. *You made some mistakes tonight, asshole. Huge ones.*

Rory didn't know what made him glance down at Olive where she sat on the floor, being comforted by her friend, but her expression caused a pause in his stride.

Her eyes were wide, her hands curled up under her chin. She looked…scared.

What did she have to be scared about? He was here. He was going to take care of everything. Take care of the idiot who'd put her in a position where she could get hurt. Rory tried to tell her that without words, but she only shook her head, fear becoming more prominent on her beautiful, but paling, face.

Olive's friend tried to block her view of Rory. And that's when Rory realized Olive was scared…of him. She was *scared* of him.

His heart plummeted to his boots so rapidly, he wondered how he remained standing. The rage drained in one fell swoop and all that remained was denial. Shame. He'd felt that combination before but never with enough force to knock the wind out of his lungs.

"Sunbeam," he mouthed, halting his progress in the direction of Polo Shirt. He forced his fists to unfold and held up both hands, approaching her slowly. "I'm sorry. I'm not going to do nothin'," he rasped, forgetting to phrase his words the right way. "Look, baby."

She sniffed hard and nodded.

Rory approached her slowly, swallowing a lump when her friend seemed reluctant to let him touch her. But Olive patted her friend's hand, never breaking eye contact once as he crouched down and replaced the glasses that had been knocked off her face. Then he scooped her up and cradled her against his chest. Bliss cascaded downward from the top of his head, traveling to his feet as he carried Olive back through the silent crowd toward the bar. Andrew passed him with a shocked expression on the way, finally shaking himself and using his authority to toss out the would-be brawlers and restore order.

Christ, it felt so good to hold her. To have her close. His need to punish the ones who'd put her in harm's way was almost squashed until he noticed the bleeding cut at her hairline. His footsteps faltered on the way into the back office. "Jamie," he said thickly. "I need the first-aid kit."

Rory barely registered his middle's brother's bewilderment before he and Olive were inside the dark office. After setting her carefully down on the edge of the desk, he used his elbow to flip on the light switch—and with Olive's beauty illuminated, he could only stare, his tongue weighted and useless in his mouth.

"You're so fucking pretty."

She gasped and sat up straighter, her chin wobbling. "Oh...*shut up*."

How many times could his heart hit the deck in one night? "Shut up?"

"That's right. Don't bring your romantic lines around here.

I'm not buying them."

"I'm not being romantic." Rory stepped closer, every cell in his body buzzing louder with every inch he traveled in her proximity. "I'm telling you what I see."

"Well, I haven't seen *you* in two weeks." She crossed her arms over her middle, but not before he saw her shudder. "I mean it, Rory. Don't act like you missed me when you could stay away so easily. Actually, I-I kind of hate you right now."

Feeling like he'd been sucker punched in the gut, he gripped the desk on either side of her thighs and leaned in as close as she would allow, smelling the air above her collarbone. "*Easily?*" He lifted his head and met her eyes. "You stayed late yesterday morning after class and missed your bus back to Long Beach. The one I follow to make sure it arrives safely?" He shook his head. "I was two seconds from heading into the Burnbaum building and finding you. You never stay late."

Her expression slowly cleared of frustration, making way for disbelief. "You've been following me?"

"Only when you travel to Stony Brook," he said, bringing their lips an inch apart, letting his thumbs graze the outside of her thighs. "I get nervous when you leave town."

"I knew it. I felt you," she whispered, eyelids fluttering. "Don't you dare kiss me, Rory Prince. I'm really mad."

There was nothing worse in the world than staying away from this girl, but having her pissed at him was a damn close second. In that moment, with the gravitational pull between them anchoring him more securely than the Earth's...he was done keeping a protective distance. Standing in front of her, having her undivided attention, was healing unseen wounds all over his body, making him whole. He needed this. He needed her.

No more staying away. He'd been lucky to make it this long.

"That kid isn't your boyfriend." Rory's breath came faster, his fingers twisting in the hem of her skirt, pure willpower stopping him from yanking her against his lap, the cock thickening behind his fly. Preparing to claim. "Is he, sunbeam?"

Olive's eyes flashed, her breath shaky as she shook her head no. "I only met him tonight. There's nothing there."

Relief adhered to him like a second layer of skin. "Good girl."

"Shut up."

Jamie chose that moment to enter, carrying the blue tin first-aid kit. In Rory's periphery, he saw his brother slow to a stop beside them, but he couldn't take his eyes off the girl sitting atop the desk. How the fuck had he managed to keep his distance?

"Whoa." Jamie laughed under his breath. "Are you going to introduce me?"

"Olive," he managed. "This is my brother, Jamie."

She put a hand on his chest to push him away, but he intercepted it and pressed his lips to the inside of her wrist instead, noting the way her pupils enlarged. Seemingly with an effort, she managed to turn her head in Jamie's direction. "It's nice to meet you," she said, smiling. "I promise I don't need whatever is in that box."

Jamie nodded once. "Up to you, Olive. You might want to let us take a quick look, though, since it's bleeding—"

"*Oh!*" Olive slid off the desk, bringing herself flush against Rory and he was forced to turn his pained face away, a moan barely subdued in his throat. "I left my friend Leanne out there. We're buddy system partners. I need to go get her."

Her obvious distress jolted Rory. "I'll go grab her." He lightly touched the cut on Olive's forehead and winced. "Will you let Jamie bandage this? Please?"

After a moment, she nodded.

"You'll be here when I get back, right?"

"Yes."

Reluctant to leave her for a second in case she disappeared, Rory kept his gaze on her as long as possible while backing out of the office. Upon reentering the bar, he saw that the summer night energy had mostly returned to normal, pitchers being hoisted, couples making out near the neon internet jukebox, cigarette smoke drifting in from outside. Andrew was swamped behind the bar, but he waved Rory off in the universal sign for *fuck off, I'll manage*. It didn't take Rory much time at all to find Leanne where she leaned on the wall near the exit, looking worried.

"You can't just carry girls off like that," was how she greeted him. "Who told you that was normal?"

Rory scratched the side of his chin and bit back a smile. "Sorry about that. I wasn't aware the buddy system was in effect."

She huffed a breath. "Is she okay?"

"Yeah. Yeah, I'm going to make sure she's okay." He jerked a thumb over his shoulder. "You want to come see for yourself?"

"No..." For the first time, Rory noticed the white smartphone she juggled from hand to hand. "She just texted me to ask if we can stay a while. But I'm going to get an Uber home. Already called one."

"Olive wants to stay, does she?" There was no stopping the kick of pleasure and anticipation from filling his belly. *Need to get back to her. Need to touch her.* He pushed open the exit with his left hand, gesturing for Leanne to precede him. "Come on, I'll walk you."

"Fine." Leanne groused. "I'll be the thing that earns your brownie points."

They walked side by side out of the bar and down the ramp of the boardwalk where Leanne's Uber was waiting. Rory made a quick mental note of the license plate, waved goodnight and turned back toward the bar, already craving the scent of Olive again. But Leanne's voice drew him up short, forcing him to look back over her shoulder.

"Why didn't you hit that guy?"

The image of Olive shrinking away from him on the bar floor hit him hard. "I was scaring her. I never want to scare her."

Leanne opened the rear door of the car. "Fighting is only one of the ways you could do that," she said tonelessly. "I hope you're paying attention."

Rory spent the walk back to the Castle Gate trying to decipher what Leanne meant, but as soon as he walked through the entrance and the promise of Olive's presence beckoned, it fled to the back of his mind. Later. He'd definitely figure it out later.

CHAPTER NINE

WHILE OLIVE TRIED not to stare at the door and wait for Rory to return with Leanne, she remained still and let Jamie swab some Neosporin onto her cut and place a small Band-Aid over the abrasion. He never touched her skin directly, and Olive got the feeling he made the effort out of respect for Rory. Right or wrong, he was possessive of her, even though he'd cut and run weeks ago. Then again…in truth, he hadn't completely bailed, had he?

Thank God her tingling flesh wasn't visible because she couldn't seem to make it stop. She should be righteously pissed that Rory had followed her bus to Stony Brook, but no matter how deep she dug down, trying to find her indignation, she couldn't locate it. Yes, that kind of behavior was unusual and…*intrusive*. But if Olive acknowledged the truth? Rory could have had her any time he wanted. Any time he chose to step out of the shadows, she would have become starved for his body heat, same as she'd done tonight in exactly three point eight seconds. He'd truly followed her to class because he was worried. After all, she'd almost walked in front of a bus, come close to drowning…and tonight she'd solidified her standing as World's Most Accident-Prone Individual. It wasn't a stretch for Rory to worry, was it?

One thing Olive knew for sure. Knowing Rory had been caring for her from a distance shouldn't be turning her on so much. Even now, when he wasn't in the room, she had to concentrate to keep her breathing even. The way he'd carried her into the office, the way he'd looked at her, like all he needed was one word of encouragement and she'd be his next meal.

I should probably stop thinking filthy thoughts with his brother literally two feet away.

Olive watched as Jamie swept the Band-Aid wrappers into his palm and tossed them into the trash. There was no denying she was curious about Rory. She'd had weak moments over the last fourteen days where she'd tried to find him on social media and failed miserably. In the world of Facebook, Instagram, Snapchat and Twitter, he didn't even exist. She had a few minutes alone with Rory's brother now. Would it be so bad to satisfy some of her curiosity while she had the chance?

"What's on your mind?" Jamie asked, before she could say a word. He lifted his head and gave her a half-smile, before posting up against the far wall. Until he struck a casual pose and crossed his arms, Olive hadn't seen a resemblance. But there it was. That head-tilting smirk Rory had employed on more than one occasion. Same green eyes, too, although Jamie's held more of a knowing twinkle, as opposed to the raw intensity of Rory's. All three of the Prince brothers were unique, yet each of them was insanely attractive. It really wasn't even fair.

Again, Jamie spoke before she got the chance. "He's probably on the way back. Get those questions in while you can."

Olive narrowed her eyes at Jamie, taking his measure. He did the same to her. Should she give him the satisfaction? Oh right, like she could help it.

But first. To lull him into a false sense of security. "Do you guys own this place?"

"Rory didn't tell you?" She shook her head. "Yeah. The three of us own the Castle Gate." Something flickered in his expression. "Took it over from my father about four years back."

She absorbed that. "And the fight that sent Rory to prison…what was it about?"

"Sorry, can't answer that one." He winked. "Has to be his choice. Nice try, though."

"Damn."

Jamie's mouth twitched, but his eyes were serious. "Believe me, I'd love to tell you, because it would help you understand him better."

"Tell me something *else* that will help me understand him."

He inclined his head. "He's been helping manage the bar for the last two weeks. Running payroll, scheduling deliveries, stocking the bar, even dabbling in online advertising. Took over for Andrew so he could focus on the beach." His expression was one of pure pride. "He's good at it, too."

Two weeks, exactly? The change couldn't have something to do with her, could it?

Jamie pointed at the office door. "I've never seen my brother back away from a fight like that. I didn't think he was physically capable of it." He raised an eyebrow. "What have you done to him?"

"I haven't been around to *do* anything. He made sure I wouldn't." She picked a piece of lint off her skirt. "I didn't even know he worked here. We're only talking right now out of pure coincidence."

"Are we?" Jamie pushed off the wall. "You guys have ended up in the same place quite a few times. Maybe it's less coincidence and more the universe trying to tell you something. And that's hard for a pragmatic economics teacher to admit."

"If it's the universe talking…I wasn't afraid to listen to it the first time." She swallowed. "But I am now. I am now that he's left before. Now that I know how it feels to watch him go."

Jamie paused near the door, a line forming between his brows. "Trust me when I say that wasn't easy for him to do," he said. "And I don't think he'll be able to do it again."

"Yeah, exactly." She gave him a half-smile. "You don't *think* so."

The door chose that moment to burst open, narrowly missing Jamie and careening off the office wall. Instead of Rory, in burst a giant man in a muscle T-shirt with a naked woman tattooed on his forearm. "What happened? Someone told me there was a fight." He deflated when he saw Jamie, doubling over and propping his hands on his knees. "Oh shit, man, when I didn't see you behind the bar I thought you'd gotten caught up in the fight." He straightened with a too-loud laugh. "So, uh. Okay. Never mind. All's well that ends well. And you're…I mean, you seem well, Jamie Prince." He scrubbed at the back of his neck. "Are you?"

"*Yes.*" Jamie pinched the bridge of his nose. "Go back to work, Marcus."

"Yup. Soon as you do." He crossed his beefy arms, the poster boy for refusing to budge. "Who's the girl? Did you change your mind about liking dudes?"

Jamie clasped his hands together. "Why yes, it's just something that happens on a whim."

Marcus squinted one eye. "Wait. Really?"

"*No.*" Jamie shoved at the man's shoulder. "Move it, dumbass. Andrew is probably ready to kill me for leaving him in the weeds this long—and before you ask—no, my brother isn't *really* ready to kill me. It's just an expression."

A beat passed. "You called me a dumbass."

Rory's brother sighed as they both passed through the doorframe. "I'm sorry, Marcus. I didn't mean it."

"Okay."

Olive was still trying to absorb both *her* conversation with Jamie, followed by the oddly endearing dynamic between him and Marcus, when Rory returned. And yeah, wow. Wow, her thighs just kind of melted into the desk and the oxygen in the room turned as thick as soup. Just like that. Olive wanted to maintain her anger at him, but she couldn't. Not when he looked so relieved to find her still there. "Where is Leanne?"

"Put her in an Uber. She's good." He reached out and caught her hand, massaging her palm with his thumb. An action Olive swore she could feel right between her legs. "Will you come out with me, sunbeam?" Rory murmured into her wrist, letting his tongue snake out and brand her skin. "There's a place down the street where everyone I know won't be watching us."

Should she do this? Open herself up for more potential disappointment and pain?

When she might have said no and let self-preservation win the day, a little reminder piped up in the back of her mind. That damning certainty that she could walk from one end of the earth to the other and no one might make her feel like Rory ever again. This time, though… she needed to keep her guard up.

"Olive?"

She took a bracing breath. "Okay, Rory. For a little while."

OLIVE HADN'T FOUND any of the bars that night particularly inspiring. Inside they all seemed to look pretty much the same. Flat-screen televisions in every corner, loud conversation, louder music, the same glowing row of jewel tone liquor bottles on the shelves. Since she'd only been inside the Castle Gate for all of two minutes before Zed picked a fight with a stranger who'd stepped on his foot, she wasn't afforded much of an opportunity to look around. As Rory led her through the crowd and out the door, however, she couldn't deny something set it apart.

The memorabilia on the walls was from another time. Sawdust decorated the floor and the aroma of it, mixed with spilled beer, made her think of some spirited, medieval gathering. There were televisions, but they weren't blaring—and one of them actually appeared to be showing classic game show reruns. A traditional Irish song ended and Radiohead began and no one seemed to notice the contrast. Olive did, though. Felt the bass and moodiness of it seep into her veins as they walked out into the cooling night.

A hunger she'd only experienced for this man thrummed in all of her erogenous zones and the nearby ocean sounds tickled her with romance. *Lust* and romance. That combination would make it especially difficult to keep up her guard. Rory pulled her into the warmth of his body, gently kissing the bandage on her head. "Poor sunbeam."

Ah geez. Safe to say she was in trouble.

"Where are we going?"

He glanced down at Olive, seeming to choose his words. "You were drinking tonight."

She made a sound of agreement. "A little."

"Did you enjoy it?"

"Kind of. I don't feel like I've found my alcohol soul mate yet, though." She made a face. "It's definitely not beer."

"You'd like a white Russian. It tastes like a milkshake."

"Are you taking me to get one?"

"No, underage drinker. I'm not." He tickled her ribs and she half laughed, half gasped at the contact. "I'm not drinking, either.

I rode my bike here tonight." His fingertips brushed up the side of her arm, then stroked back down. "Normally that wouldn't keep me from having a beer, but not tonight. Not when I'm driving you home."

Her stomach flipped. "I get to ride on it?"

Rory pulled her to a stop at the boardwalk railing and they faced each other, slow, sticky heat meandering down her breasts and belly. They gravitated closer as if unable to help it and Olive's head tipped back until the ends of her hair tickled her shoulder blades. He wanted to kiss her, she could see it. Her mouth softened at a moment's notice, but the kiss never came, despite their obvious need of it.

"Does the idea of riding on my bike make you nervous?"

With anyone else? Absolutely. With this man? She couldn't imagine a scenario where he'd allow a hair on her head to be harmed. "No. I'm not nervous." Still not ready to let him off the hook for the last two weeks, she tried to pull off a casual shrug. "I saw you on the bike today. At a stoplight. You seemed to handle it proficiently, I guess."

He reared back a touch. "You saw me. Where?"

"Outside that coffee shop on East Park Avenue." She rolled her lips inward to wet them. "I was on the fence about whether to come out tonight, but when I saw you just going about your business, I said yes. I was finished waiting for a call that would never come." She shook her head. "Why am I telling you this?"

"Because you want to torture me," he rasped. True to his words, his expression was pained as he pressed his lips to her forehead, brushing a kiss there. "I'm sorry."

Olive hummed, digging her fingernails into her palms to keep from tracing every inch of his body with her hands. Tugging him closer and anchoring herself with his heat, like she yearned to do.

"The kids you were with tonight…" He caught her hair where it flew around in the wind, holding it in a light fist. "You go to school with those guys?"

"Stop calling them kids. Most of them are older than me."

A single eyebrow went up. "Want to know what I'd prefer to call them?"

"No," she said quickly, battling a smile. "Yes, we go to school together—and once again for the cheap seats, you don't have the right to be jealous."

His eyelids fell to half-mast. "Oh no?"

"Nope."

Rory's mouth dropped to hers without warning, pushing, his upper lip curling against hers. Their breath collided and hastened, his fingers slipping into her hair and gripping. "It's not like this with anyone else. For either of us. Is it?"

Olive shook her head once, quickly, in a hurry to get back to their almost kiss. "No."

"I want the right to be jealous, Olive. I'm working on it. While I get there, let's not pretend this thing between us follows the usual rules. It doesn't." He kissed her hard. No tongue. Just an unrelenting suction of lips desperate for contact from which he pulled back way too soon, his breathing labored. "I don't notice girls anymore. Not for weeks. There's only one."

"Good," she heard herself say, the word emerging from some deep, earthy part of her.

"Exactly. Good. That's what you want, whether or not it's supposed to be too soon."

Kiss me. Kiss me. Kiss me. "Yes."

"Because there are no fucking rules for us. So I'm going to wake up in a cold sweat tonight thinking of that kid's arm around you."

"His name is Zed and I couldn't stand him."

Rory puffed a laugh and rolled their foreheads together. "Good girl."

They stayed that way for long moments, swaying side to side, their mouths hovering so close she could taste the mint on his breath. His thumbs massaged her scalp. It was exactly where she wanted to be, even though every second with Rory seemed to hold a fine edge of uncertainty. He was so unpredictable. Every action, every word, his thoughts. She couldn't even predict *herself* around him. Yet at the same time, she wouldn't budge from that spot on the boardwalk if a meteor was hurtling toward earth.

"Even though I couldn't stand him, I'm glad you didn't fight tonight," she whispered. "I'm proud of you for stopping."

Rory melted into her, pushing his face into the crook of her neck. Inhaling. "Yeah?"

"Uh huh."

"Turns out the one thing worse than watching you fall down is seeing you scared of me. Really scared. Like you didn't know me."

"I wasn't scared of you, Rory. I was scared *for* you."

He lifted his head, searching her face with a questioning expression.

Olive gave in to her impulses, sliding her hands up beneath his T-shirt and resting them on his chest, thrilling at the way his heart kicked into an erratic rhythm under her palms. "When you told me about the man you put in the hospital, you were so sad. I don't think you *like* fighting. I was scared tonight of you doing something else you'd regret." Her fingernails moved in a light circle over his heart. "You got it backwards. I was looking at you like I *knew* you."

Rory stared down at her. "If you keep looking at me just like this, I'll never use my fists again." Finally, he rode his open mouth over hers, letting their tongues flick together, dance away and stroke back, the kiss deepening on a mutual groan. Olive's back was pressed to the boardwalk rail, Rory's right arm sliding between the barrier and her hips, urging her up and into the cradle of his body. When her tummy met the stiffness behind the fly of his jeans, she broke the kiss on a gasp, her head falling back and allowing Rory to raze the curve of her neck with his teeth, his forearm yanking her up on her toes. Closer, close as humanly possible.

"*Rory.*"

His mouth traveled lower and Olive felt damp heat through the thin silk of her tank top, right over her nipple. Felt his lips close around the bud, a male groan vibrating her head to toe. His hair was a mess by the time their mouths were level again, his eyes glazed. "Yeah, baby?"

Olive gathered her courage and reached for the thing she needed more than oxygen in that moment. Him. Them. Alone. "Do you have the ingredients at your house to make me a white Russian?"

A small fraction of the lust displayed on his face was replaced by hesitancy—and Olive's stomach twisted at the proof that he was still not a hundred percent into this. *Them.* Still thought she was too young, he was too wrong. Too bad. That his past had caused too much damage. Whatever the reason, her guard was already shooting back into place to prevent the inevitable hurt—

"Yeah. I've got the ingredients to make a *minor* a drink." With a dry half-smile, he twined their fingers together and tugged her toward the boardwalk steps, which led to the sidewalk and the town beyond. "Come on, sunbeam. Let's go break the law."

CHAPTER TEN

RORY INHALED DEEPLY and held his breath, just so Olive's fingertips would bite into his chest. Fuck, it felt amazing. Her thighs were wrapped around his hips and the purr of his bike's engine caused just enough friction to poke holes in his self-control. Thank God, too. Lust was distracting him from the possibility of getting in an accident. They were only riding fifteen blocks and he'd given her his helmet. At nearly one in the morning, the avenues were quiet. He'd never been in so much as a scrape on his bike. And yet, there was a fine layer of sweat on his skin over having the responsibility of Olive holding on to him for her safety, his eyes straining while searching for potholes or jaywalkers on the road ahead.

Was he actually bringing Olive home?

Forget the fact that the Prince bachelor pad needed a serious facelift and Olive was probably used to much finer surroundings. He was more worried about what happened when they arrived. Would she stay the night?

Rory's molars ground together as blood rushed below his belt. Jesus, he hadn't forgotten over the last two weeks what it was like to kiss Olive, but he must have suppressed the full experience of it so he wouldn't lose his mind while staying away from her. When her mouth opened beneath his, the rush was potent enough to clear his mind of anything but getting more. Absorbing the texture of her mouth, the flesh under his hands. His sole purpose became giving and taking and giving and taking until normal functions like breathing became an afterthought. She *was* breathing.

A large part of Rory still warned him to stay away from Olive. She was the kind of girl a man worked a lifetime to keep. He'd only been busting his ass for two weeks. That was *nothing*. He'd done nothing to deserve the trusting hands molded to his chest. The stigma of his past choices would always follow him around and, in turn, Olive, if they stayed together.

If they stayed together?

Rory laughed silently and without humor. He hadn't really let her go in the first place, had he? Following her to class, riding past her building on the off chance he'd catch a glimpse. Now they'd found their way back into one another's lives and she would probably spend the night in his bed. They were together. There was no going back.

Not for him.

He would die before putting that kind of pressure on her, though. This intelligent girl with the fucking world at her disposal, as it should be.

So Rory made a deal with himself. One that made his throat tighten and fear of the unknown take root. He'd allow himself to have Olive. He'd give her everything he knew how. If she decided someday that it wasn't enough, he'd force himself to accept it.

Rory was still having a hard time swallowing as they pulled up in front of the house. He climbed off the bike, unhooking the helmet strap carefully from beneath her chin, his fingers unusually clumsy because he couldn't concentrate around that smile.

"That was…"

"What?"

"Addictive," she breathed, running her hands over the body

of his bike. "I want one."

"No."

"Excuse me?"

Rory wrapped his hands around Olive's waist and plucked her off the bike. "Do we need reminding about the walking in front of a bus incident? How about your near-drowning experience?" He took her hand and led her up the stoop to his front door, which he unlocked with a quick twist of the keys. "Now you've got a gash on your head. My heart can't take it, sunbeam. Don't do me like this."

"Sorry. I'm duty bound as a woman to get a motorcycle now because a man told me no." She gave him a pitying look. "I already decided on a red one."

"*Olive*," he growled, picking her up as they entered the kitchen. She squealed and twisted in his arms, leaving their bodies melded together and her feet off the ground. He opened his mouth to tell her once again, in no uncertain terms, he'd watch her ride a motorcycle over his dead body. Instead, he said, "Why don't I teach you how to ride mine and we'll see how it goes?

Her smile sent his heart up into his mouth. "You'll really teach me?"

"Yeah." God, he had it so fucking bad. "You're already going to be the death of me. Just make sure you're not the death of *you*, too."

There they were again, their bodies straining to get closer, their mouths poised in that just about to kiss position, chests beginning to heave. Rory's dick was in full protest mode, making its argument for instant gratification with a torturous throb. He could kiss her now, but he wouldn't be able to stop...and God help him, he actually wanted to take it slow. *Take it slow.* Rory wasn't sure he'd ever played that phrase in his head before, let alone spoken it aloud.

So be it. He'd just come home to an empty house with the girl who ruled his every waking thought. They were surrounded in quiet and all time restraints had faded away, making them two people coming home from a long day. Kind of like playing house, except his intentions were far more adult in nature. Simply put, he wanted the experience of witnessing Olive in his kitchen, in his staircase. Wanted to hear her footsteps on the floorboards.

Reluctantly, he eased Olive to her feet with a kiss to the forehead. "Want me to show you around?"

"Sure," she murmured, visibly shaking herself. "Yes."

He laced their fingers together, unable to stop himself from kissing her knuckles, brushing them with his thumb. "There's a front door, but we never use it. We just come in through the kitchen."

"What is that?" She pointed at the big, dented steel container sitting on the counter beside the stove.

"Those are Jiya's spices." He led her over to the metal drum and popped off the lid, revealing the compartments within. "These are kind of the staple Indian spices. Black mustard seeds, dried chili pepper, hardar—that's turmeric powder—and a cumin coriander mixture." He smiled. "If it weren't for her, we'd probably eat nothing but takeout. She makes us help, though, so we're getting better. I can make khichdi now without looking at the recipe."

She leaned in and sniffed the spices. "I don't think I've ever had it."

"I'll be your first."

Olive's eyes shot to his, drifting low to his mouth. Pink climbed her neck and Rory barely resisted following that color change with his tongue. "Um, speaking of firsts…" Olive said huskily. "I believe I'm owed a white Russian."

Rory sighed through a smile. "I was hoping you'd forget."

She leaned a hip against the counter. "You're really in a moral quandary over giving me one alcoholic beverage?"

"Yeah." After dragging a hand through his hair, he reached into the cabinet above the stove and took out their resident bottle of Absolut vodka. "I really am."

"I'm in college. It's the designated time for drunken revelry."

Rory took a clean glass out of the dishwasher and filled it with ice from the fridge. He measured out vodka, Kahlua and milk, then dumped all the contents into a martini shaker, watching her through narrowed eyes as he mixed and cooled the ingredients. "I made it light."

She kept her attention on his face as he transferred the icy, light brown concoction back into the glass. "You know," she started. "If we're going to…"

"What?"

The pink climbed from her neck to her cheeks, making her skin flushed and even more sexy than usual. "Well, if I'm d-dating someone who works at a bar, I'll probably have a drink once in a while, right?"

His cock grew uncomfortably heavy over the word *dating*. *I'm going to take this girl on dates. Bring her home afterward. Have her all to myself.* Was this even reality? "Yeah, you probably will," he said, his voice low. After a moment's hesitation, he slid her the drink across the counter. "Sometimes I equate alcohol with bad decisions. My own, especially. But you helped me make a good one tonight and…I just want to do the same for you. As often as I can."

Her gray eyes were inquisitive, always reading between the lines. "You've probably seen a lot of people make bad decisions in the bar." A beat passed wherein he said nothing. "What about at home?"

Rory tried to clear the sudden clutter in his throat. "My dad drank some," he said, turning away to put the bottles back in their places. "A lot, actually."

"Where is he now?"

"We don't know," Rory answered, still unable to look at her. "My mother is in Bayside, though. Living with her sister back in Queens where she grew up," he said, trading one uncomfortable subject for another. He couldn't seem to keep himself from telling Olive the shit in his head, though. Not when she projected total understanding and a lack of judgment that made him forget things like secrets and uncomfortable truths. "Her birthday is next week, actually."

Olive studied him. "Are you going?"

Rory shook his head. "I never go. I…can't." Finished with his task of putting away the bottles and closing the cabinets, he stuck his hands on his hips. Breathed in and out. "I haven't gone to see her since everything happened. Since I went away when I was eighteen. So I've missed more than a couple."

"That's a long time." She slipped her hand around the cocktail but made no move to pick it up. "Why do you stay away?"

As always, when he thought of his mother, he remembered the look on her face in the courtroom the day he was sentenced. She'd raised three boys and lived with an abusive husband, so she'd known disappointment well. Still, he'd never seen it line her face more deeply than it had that day. "Jamie and Andrew weren't living in the house when it happened. I was the only one left here with my parents. I could run interference with my father. Make sure I was home when he was drinking and feeling mean. He'd stopped putting his hands on her by then or he knew what would happen." Rory rubbed at the ache in his sternum, but the friction only made it worse. "There was nothing to stop him once I was put away, Olive. I can't believe I left her alone with him. If I'd been there, I would have saved her."

"Rory," she whispered, her face pained. "I'm so sorry for your mother. No one should have to live in fear like that. But you can't punish yourself for something that happened so long ago. Even if you hadn't gone away, you couldn't have stayed here forever. I don't know your mother, but I'm sure she wouldn't have wanted to put the responsibility of protecting her on you. Not indefinitely. It wouldn't have been fair." Olive kept coming toward him until she laid her head on his chest, wrapping her arms around his waist. "You've been feeling guilty enough to stay away for six years. If you ever tell me again you're a bad guy, I'm going to…to…"

Rory tried to be quiet about letting go of the breath he'd been holding. "What, sunbeam?"

"Pout. I'll pout."

Jesus. Rory had never felt lighter in his life. He'd just told this girl the ugly truth about his family and how he'd been carrying the responsibility for his mother's pain…and she seemed to have found something beautiful in the midst of so much ugly. She hadn't even taken the time to think about whether or not he was to blame, simply declaring he wasn't. God, how tempting it was to believe her, but he'd been packed to the gills with regret and guilt for so long, he could only let a small degree of it go. "How will you pout? Show me."

She tilted her head back so Rory could see her duck lips and thunderous frown. "How is this? Are you scared?"

"Ah, baby. I'm terrified."

Olive smiled and planted a kiss over his heart. The gesture

started casual, but they made eye contact while her lips were still pressed to the spot and the atmosphere changed. There was an awareness on Olive's face that said she heard the wild rapping of that organ against his rib cage. Both of their breathing changed and in an instant, the closeness of their bodies was no longer meant to comfort.

"I'll go to the birthday party with you," Olive murmured, shifting her sweet curves against him. "If you want."

A knot formed in his throat. "You would do that for me?"

She nodded. "Promise."

Trying to disguise how much that offer humbled him, Rory swallowed hard, reaching over to pick up the drink he'd made and holding it to her lips. "Take a sip. I'm not going to inflict my hang-ups on you. Ever. Understand?" When Olive nodded and did as she was told, watching him silently over the rim of the glass, he was jealous over the cool liquid that met and slid across her tongue, down her throat. Fuck, just watching her take the sip made his balls feel twice their usual weight. If he didn't kiss her soon, he was going to go mad. She licked her lips after she'd taken her fill, and Rory cinched his hips forward, just enough to inform her of the effect she had. Constantly. Her lids fluttered, her pupils blocking out some of the gray of her irises, and she murmured his name like a prayer.

Rory set the glass down and plowed his hands into her hair, holding fast as he walked her backward toward the staircase. The one that led to his bedroom. Even as a voice in the back of his head reminded him he wasn't good enough to be Olive's first time, the gravitational pull between them wasn't giving him a choice. He needed her. He *needed her*. But his conscience forced him to offer one more out. One more, before he lost sight of the right thing to do.

"I can bring you home," he rasped, grazing their lips together. "Just say the word."

Olive's breath caught as she scrutinized him, the importance of what could happen once they got upstairs written in her eyes. Probably his, too. "I'm staying."

CHAPTER ELEVEN

OLIVE WAS READY to get naked before they reached the top of the stairs.

Pretty intrepid for a girl who'd only gone as far as kissing with a member of the opposite sex—and some on-top-of-the-clothes groping once at church camp, but it had been so unskilled and awkward, she'd stricken it from the record. Rory would not be unskilled. One need only to examine the facts to arrive at such a conclusion.

Oh God, did she mentally monologue in essay format when she was turned on? Whatever. It was helping keep her focused. And she wanted to remember every single moment of tonight. So. Facts.

He wasn't rushed. Hadn't even kissed her yet, merely walking her into the dark bedroom and breathing against her lips. Breathing, rubbing their mouths together, humming. Stroking her hair and every so often reminding her of the raised flesh behind his fly. This wasn't a young, inexperienced guy with his orgasm on a hair trigger. He was seducing her even though there was no need. She'd been seduced the morning they'd shared milkshakes.

Rory ran his thumbs in hook patterns behind her ears, massaging the spots she didn't even know were sensitive. What else did he know about her body she didn't? When she woke up tomorrow morning, what secrets would she have learned?

Excitement raced up and down her arms like spiky pinwheels, clashing with nerves to leave her trembling, breathless.

He made her breathless. This man who carried so much weight on his shoulders. She wanted to take it away from him, distract him from it for as long as possible. Remembering his tortured expression back in the kitchen, the sharp ache in her chest flared to life again. He'd been through so much—and while she still didn't know the extent of it, she knew a man who lamented letting down his mother to such a degree was good at his core. And Olive could feel the truth of his goodness with every treasuring caress of her skin, every awed glance he sent in her direction. She was going to give herself to this man, wholeheartedly, because staying away was impossible. Painful, even.

Please, please don't let me regret it.

Don't let me find out again what it's like to see him go.

Wanting to forget her remaining reservations about the future, Olive wet her lips, her voice emerging in a smoky croak. "Um, so. Are you planning on kissing me soon?"

He made a low sound in his throat, just as the back of her legs met the edge of the mattress. "Not yet, baby."

"Oh." The husky way he said *baby* caused moisture to gather between her thighs, making the thin material of her panties cling. "Why?"

Rory pressed their foreheads together. "You get so hot when we kiss. Trying to climb me and letting out those sexy, little whimper sounds." He unwound his fingers from her hair, dropping them to her hips and squeezing. "I'm already hard as a fucking rock for you, Olive. Going slow is probably going to kill me, but my mind is set. I'm giving you the best I've got."

The threads of yearning and determination in his tone made her nod jerkily. Made her understand. Rory *needed* to make tonight special, just as much as she needed it to be. Just this once, she needed to trust that someone else's experience trumped her always-at-the-ready logic, the belief she knew what was best for herself. Just for tonight, she would trust *Rory* to know and give her exactly what she needed.

"On the bed," he whispered in her ear. "Want to hold you for a while."

Olive almost sobbed at being denied more kissing, but remembering her resolve to let Rory guide them, she sat down on the bed and scooted toward the headboard. Though the interior of the room was dark, the moonlight coming in through the single window allowed her to watch Rory render himself shirtless and prowl toward her like a sleek, tattooed animal on the mattress. When she swore he was going to climb on top of her—and prayed he would—he carefully removed her glasses and set them on his nightstand. Then he dropped down beside Olive, turned her body and spooned her from behind.

His heavy forearm draped over her hip, and after a slight hesitation, he drew her back and pressed her backside *tighttighttight* to his lap, releasing a long groan into her ear. "This ass of yours is ruining my life, baby, you know that? So high and sweet it hurts." His tongue dragged down the slope of her neck, his teeth razing her shoulder. "Every part of you. *Every* part is so beautiful, I can't think straight. Can't decide what to appreciate first. Do I want to wrap your thighs around my head? Or just get those incredible eyes on me and fucking *live* there, because I should be grateful you're looking at me in the first place? It's a goddamn struggle, sunbeam. You don't even know."

The pressure Rory always created in her chest multiplied in strength now, pushing outward, robbing her of oxygen. Needing to get as close as humanly possible, she curled her foot around his calf, tucked her head back into the notch of his throat. "It's the same for me. I want to do anything for you," she rambled, her eyes closed. "I want to do anything *with* you. Maybe it was too soon? I-I don't know, but it hurt so bad when you went away."

"I'm sorry," he grated into Olive's hair, yanking her closer, ever closer, dislodging her foot when he slung a muscular thigh over both of hers. "God, I'm so fucking sorry."

She shook off the niggling fear of it happening again and changed the subject, refusing to dwell there when they were finally together like this. "Touch me, Rory. Please?"

What happened next was the most erotic moment of her life. Which was saying something considering this man had performed oral on her in a public shower. Rory's fingertips slid slowly, slowly down her hip, moving beneath the high hem of her skirt. His breathing turned shallow at the back of her neck as he drew up the garment, inch by inch. Air kissed the flesh of Olive's bare backside and she dug her fingers into the flannel bedcovers, feeling his hot perusal of what he'd displayed. A blunt digit tucked under the thin strip of her thong, running back and forth, the action causing his knuckle to drag through the split of her bottom—and oh boy. Still mostly clothed and she was already learning secrets about her body, because she'd had no clue a man's touch *there* was supposed to feel good. No, *amazing*.

"*Rory*—"

"Give me a minute," he gritted out, that knuckle continuing it's back and forth journey, his breath hot on her neck. "I know you'll go out with friends once in a while, Olive. I want you to. But can you save the short skirt and thong combo for nights out with Rory? Huh?"

His possessiveness should have been a turn-off. Right? Lord, it was *not*. Not even a little bit. It made her feel feminine and powerful and protected all at once. "I was hoping I'd see you." Halfway through that revelation, Rory let the strap of her thong snap lightly between her buns and Olive saw stars, forcing her to break off in a gasp. "I didn't expect to, but—"

Rory's mouth suctioned hard to the side of her neck, his big hand gripping her right butt cheek in a rough massage. "Do we have a deal, baby?" His tongue licked over the spot on her neck where he'd definitely left a mark. "When it's this easy for someone to get their hands on your beautiful ass, I want to be with you. Because that won't be happening. Not unless it's me." He squeezed hard enough to make her sob. "Only these hands touch you here. Everywhere. My life flashed in front of my fucking eyes when I saw that guy's arm around your shoulders, so I'm going to be a bastard about this one thing, Olive. Please. Make the deal."

"No thong and short skirt combo when I go out," she hiccupped, pressing back into his touch, craving more of it the more she was given. "Not unless you're with me. I promise."

"Good girl." Before she could guess his intentions, Rory rolled Olive onto her back and slid down low on the bed, putting his mouth on level with her sex. His expression was focused and hungry as he stripped off her thong, exposing her for only a second before his tongue found her in a teasing lick that parted her wet folds. "Now I'll show you my end of the deal," he said thickly, kissing the lips between her thighs in the same manner he would her mouth. "Keep this all for me and I'll make sure it's always satisfied."

Rory's calloused fingers made a V to keep her open for his mouth, and with eyelids at half-mast, he dragged the flat of his tongue over her clit, back and forth, side to side. *Side to side.* Olive's vision wavered, a cry of his name sticking in her throat.

Lights winked on the ceiling of Rory's bedroom briefly resembling the big dipper, her fingers tangling in his hair. Rory almost knocked her hold on the strands free when he slung her thighs over his broad shoulders, but Olive held fast, whimpering at the new angles the position made available.

"*Goddamn*, baby. So wet," Rory growled, his shoulders flexing underneath her thighs, his hips shifting against the edge of the bed. "I spend every second of the day wanting to eat you up for a good reason. Your pussy is a drug. *My* fucking drug."

A hard shudder went through Olive's body. She'd always pictured her first time as a necessary evil. A gateway to eventual better things. But here she was, grinding herself onto Rory's giving tongue, pulling his face closer, babbling incoherently up at the stars that continued to wink on the ceiling. Her thighs alternated between a melted butter sensation and bow-tight quickening, her throat straining with the need to scream. Better wasn't possible. "Oh my God. S-*stop*. I'm going to…"

Rory's thumb tucked just inside her entrance, rubbing at the flesh beyond. "You're going to come? Good." His eyes were glazed and hot, fastened to Olive's face as he flickered his tongue against her clit, once, twice. "That's what happens when I lick your pussy, baby. Just give in."

A tether snapped inside of Olive and a hot river of relief tore through her, throwing her back up into an arch, her fingers tearing at Rory's hair. His mouth was no longer teasing, no longer finessing. No, he was greedy. While her private flesh seized, released, seized, he lapped at her, making low sounds in his throat, as if he couldn't get enough of her taste. That visible enjoyment prolonged Olive's orgasm until her sides started to throb with the strain.

When her vision cleared, Rory was above her, his harsh,

handsome face shadowed, his hair a wreck from her desperate fingers. "We can stop now," he said on a shaking exhale and Olive saw he'd unfastened his pants, one hand out of sight inside the loosened denim, forearm flexing, flexing, as he stroked himself. "I can stop," he rasped, as if trying to convince himself.

"No," she breathed, physically aching with the need to have their skin pressed together. So much so that she whipped her tank top off, her shaking fingers fumbling with the front snap of her strapless bra. "Come here. Please? Come…"

Rory laid his warm hand on top of hers, lowering his mouth and distracting her with a kiss as he undid her bra, pushing the silky cups aside and palming her right breast. She could feel the weight of his erection drop to her bare belly, full and hard.

"I want you on top of me," she said in a thready rush.

She couldn't decipher his exact expression. It had notes of wonder, disbelief and deep sexual frustration. But it was intense enough to stall the rapid filling and emptying of her lungs. Rory braced his forearms on either side of her and eased down, giving Olive his weight little by little, both of them moaning at the contact. "*Jesus Christ*," he groaned into her neck. "You're wrecking me, sunbeam."

Olive hadn't known the meaning of the word *decadence* until that moment. Or at the very least, she'd always associated it with chocolate. There was nothing more decadent on the planet than having Rory's weight pressing her down into the soft mattress, though. His skin was hot and fragrant with his distinct male scent, cut with the sharpness of liquor and fruit, probably because he'd been handling both at the bar. She could feel every shift of muscle in his abdomen, chest, thighs. Needing more—*more*—Olive slid her thighs wider and hooked her knees around Rory's legs, conforming the arches of her feet to his calf muscles.

While she was busy reveling in the various textures of Rory, his breath was turning more and more shallow in her neck, his hips beginning to grind down, pushing the hard length of his arousal into her pelvis. His mouth opened beneath her ear, pressing seeking kisses to the ultra-sensitive spot. "You're so sexy," he whispered, laving her with his tongue. "So beautiful. So fucking beautiful. Can't believe I'm with you like this."

She dragged her palms down the ridges of his back, straight into the loose waistband of his jeans, past the barrier of his boxer briefs. When her hands elevated and slid over the smooth curves of his ass, the decadence reached an even higher peak, because Rory made it obvious he liked her hands there. Liked having her hands anywhere. "I want you inside me," she murmured, letting her nails score his buttocks lightly, then with more insistence as he panted. "Rory, please." Olive lifted her hips and tugged his lower body closer at the same time. "I can feel how bad you need me."

A vibration ran the length of him. "S'never going to go away," he half-slurred in her ear, before dragging his mouth down her neck, over her cleavage, where he licked a nipple into his mouth, his hips punching against her on the first suck. "Be sure, Olive. Are you sure?"

"Yes," she moaned as he switched breasts. "I want you. Now."

Rory surged over her, stopping to kiss her mouth hard, before reaching for his bedside table. He took a foil packet out of the drawer and ripped it open with his teeth, his hand vanishing between them to cover his erection. Olive's relentless curiosity made her anxious to watch the process, but there would be ample time for that later. Watching the pucker of Rory's forehead and the sweat beading on his upper lip was far more enjoyable. He was suffering. Going through hell in his hunger to be inside her body—how amazing was that? It was even more amazing that she could end that pain, simply by giving her own body what it cried out for. Contact. Rory. Relief. Intimacy with this man.

He didn't push inside her right away. No, he dropped his forehead to Olive's and rolled it side to side, eyes closed, as if in denial. She was prepared to beg again, to fight against whatever obstacles he'd inflated between them in his mind. In the end, there was no need, though. Rory fastened his mouth to hers and trailed a hand down her stomach, taking hold of his thick sex, rubbing the big head through her wealth of moisture.

"Give me the words, sunbeam," he said, his eyes arrested on her face. "Ask for what you want by name."

She shuddered as his flesh glided over her clit, circling it. "You, I want you."

"What do you want from me?" He pushed the tip of his erection inside of Olive, his jaw losing power as he groaned. "What do you want from this cock?"

God above, was she supposed to love it so much when he said that word? Olive licked her parched lips and arched her back, showing him her breasts and watching his eyes glaze. "I want to…" She reached for the basest truth she could find. "I want to watch you enjoy me. Enjoy…fucking m-me. I want you to give yourself an orgasm with my body."

Rory made a hoarse sound and tucked another inch inside of her. Another. Olive's knees shot up automatically as discomfort threatened, but Rory's kiss blurred everything. *Everything.* All she could feel and think about was the slow, wet mating of their tongues, the savoring scrapes of sound in his throat as the kiss turned deeper, deep enough that she grew dizzy, giddiness tickling her ribs…and her thighs dropped open once more.

"You left out the part about you coming again, baby," Rory

murmured in between mind-numbing kisses. "We fuck, you come. It's a given, you understand?"

Feeling hypnotized by a pair of intense, green eyes, she nodded. "Yes."

"I'm going deeper now," he groaned, rocking his hips forward and letting loose a string of curses over her head. "Olive. Olive. You're too tight. You're *so tight.*"

The sudden pressure wrenched a sob from Olive's throat. Moisture pricked the backs of her eyelids. It was more the shock of being filled for the first time than actual pain. And the satisfaction of having Rory's body locked together with her own was so powerful and right, she wanted to lean into the minor ache. Embrace it.

"Baby." Rory studied her face, concern etched between his dark brows. "Ah, baby, are you okay?" He made a visible effort to swallow a growl, but it emerged anyway, his hips seeming to plow forward of their own volition. "Oh my God, Olive. *Christ.* You feel incredible."

"You feel so good, too," she said, awed, shifting her lower body around so she could memorize every new sensation. "So hard, Rory."

He barked a humorless laugh, the muscles in his shoulders and chest bunching. "I can't hold still when you say things like that."

Olive's hands traveled down his strong back to settle once again on the swells of his ass. "Don't. Don't hold still."

Right before her eyes, the final traces of Rory's control evaporated and he fell on top of her like a starving man. His mouth moved over hers like it held the secrets of the universe, their tongues twining, his flesh leaving her and pumping back in, slow and deep, slow and deep, the erotic rhythm writing itself on her soul instantaneously. The root of his erection ground against her hyper-sensitive clit with such incessant friction, Olive couldn't stay still. Her thighs circled Rory's hips, hugging them tight, her hips lifting to meet his thrusts. She didn't know where the desire for *hard* and *fast* came from, only that it was there. And *undeniable*. When she couldn't find relief right away, she dropped her legs from around Rory's body and spread them wide, wide, swallowing a strangled moan when his cock bore down, exploiting her nub of flesh while he watched her from above. *There.* There it was.

"My brothers won't be home for hours, baby," Rory gritted, his pace going from methodical to anxious. Hungry. Desperate. "Scream your little heart out."

And she did. He angled his body to rub her more thoroughly and she let a scream rip, her fingernails burying themselves in his tight butt cheeks, holding him fast. Keeping him there.

He caught her jaw in his right hand, tilting it up and hovering his mouth right above hers—*right above*—watching her every reaction like a hawk. "Do you have any idea how fucking perfect you feel?" His thumb tugged her lower lip down, then slipped all the way into her mouth. "God, a man like me should have to sell his soul to be your first, but you're giving yourself to me. Saving me. You're *saving* this black soul." He pulled his thumb from her mouth, spreading the wetness over her lips while watching in fascination. "What the hell did I do to deserve you?"

Olive wanted to tell him he didn't have to do a single thing to deserve her. He only needed to be his exact self. Just Rory. The man who carried unnecessary pain and tried to save her from himself, even though they were meant to be just like this. Together. And she hoped she conveyed that with her eyes before he dropped his face into the crook of her neck and began bucking into her in rough strokes, his broken grunts filling her ears, turning her on to the nth degree.

Finally being given that hard, fast, unfettered sex she'd been craving without even knowing how it felt, Olive's eyes rolled into the back of her head, her thighs shooting together to ride on Rory's driving hips. Now she knew. She knew being the object of lust was glorious when you shared that same lust for the man. The mounting pressure in Rory's body was obvious in his frantic movements, the way he reached between them to tease her clit with the pads of his fingers. He wasn't long for this world and his touch demanded she come along for the flight up, up and away.

"Swollen, little virgin clit. So confused how it got that way," he muttered hoarsely into her hair. He reached back and gripped the underside of her knees, yanking them high around his hips and grinding her down into the mattress, his flesh entering her with wet slaps. "Going to come inside you now like God intended. Want you with me. *Be with me*, baby."

His words pushed her across the finish line, almost as much as the moist friction of their lower bodies. A ticklish tightening in her loins signaled the end and she barreled toward it, her orgasm made brighter and sharper from the knowledge that Rory was going to climax. God, the cords of his throat stood out, his mouth open, eyes blind…and she watched him go over the edge with her name on his lips. It was too quick. It went on forever. She didn't know. Didn't know, but witnessing Rory's pleasure was the single most incredible moment of her life. He went from being rocked with tension to being completely devoid of it, collapsing on top of her on the bed, gathering her so close in his arms, she could barely breathe.

Moments later, when Rory lifted his head and searched her eyes, she couldn't stop the most brilliant smile from spreading across her mouth. He returned it.

And Olive Cunningham fell completely and irreversibly in love with Rory Prince.

CHAPTER TWELVE

What's your favorite color slime? Answer below in the comments and don't forget to like and subscribe! If you enjoyed this challenge, there are tons more…

Panic trickled into Olive's veins as her eyelids cracked open, allowing the morning light to reach in and blind her. Which didn't help her total disorientation one bit. The sounds that had typically reached her ears over the last few weeks were ocean waves crashing, metal store fronts opening, joggers chatting as they ran past her building. Not her parents and siblings and giggling, muffled by her bedroom door. Had she dreamed moving to Long Beach? Had she dreamed Rory?

Olive's heart dropped into her stomach at the thought and she cracked an eye open once again, praying she would find herself lying on flannel sheets that smelled of man and musk. No way she could dream so elaborately. No way she could dream someone so complicated and beautiful, could she?

Tune back in next week when we'll be building a spider web in the backyard and having a family laser tag party. You don't want to miss it! Like and subscribe…

Please no. *Please…*

The sun shining through the window dimmed briefly and the outline of Rory came into view. And her heart shifted back into place but made no move to resume its normal rhythm. He was shirtless, standing across the room, sweatpants slung low around his hips, rubbing a towel over his wet hair. Tattoos clung to his skin the way she'd done last night, blacks and blues and a hint of red here and there. God, so hot. So insanely, ridiculously, movie-star-quality hot. There was a line of concentration between his brows, and Olive finally realized where the familiar sounds of family bonding were coming from. Rory's laptop was open on his dresser. He was watching a *Meet the Cunninghams* video?

Trying to ignore the discomfort that rippled through her chest, Olive sat up slowly. "Um. Why are you watching that?"

Rory turned to her with a casual smirk, as if about to make a dry remark, but whatever he saw on her face caused him to slam the laptop shut, concern blanketing his expression. "Hey. I...shit, sunbeam. I'm an idiot." He dropped the towel and crawled toward her on the bed, hitting her nose with clean, soapy, male goodness. "I woke up a while ago and I started worrying..." A beat passed as he shook his head. "Three bachelors live here and we almost never clean. It was never any great shakes to begin with, but we've kind of destroyed it over the years. You must be used to much nicer. I was kind of torturing myself by finding out the kind of house you grew up in. But I didn't think it would be torture for you." He pressed her back into the pillows with a long, slow kiss. "I'm sorry."

"It's okay," she whispered, her body screaming to life beneath the sheets. "Why are you up so early? It's Sunday."

In the short space of time it took them to kiss, his pupils had bled completely into his green irises. "I'm prepping the bar now almost every day. I have to go marry the liquor bottles, stock the shelves, do some paperwork." He made a harsh sound. "Of course, as soon as I volunteer for the job, I've got a reason for never wanting to leave this bed."

"That's quite a coincidence."

"No. Not a coincidence," he said quietly, laying his lips along her right cheek. "You're the reason I volunteered for the job. The reason I wanted more responsibility." His mouth trailed lightly across her mouth to lay a feathery kiss on her left cheek. "See, I don't deserve you. And I'm not even sure I was aware of what I was doing…but I know now. I was trying—I *am* trying to earn you a little at a time. I just want to *earn* you."

Olive had to bite her tongue to keep from blurting *I love you*. That wet, melting sensation was back between her thighs, her mouth was dry, her heart was rapping against her ribs. God, she was a complete mess over this man and he thought he had to earn her? "Rory—"

"Olive." Rory brushed her hair back from her face, a harsh laugh scraping out of his mouth. "Do you have any idea how fucking cute you look right now? Hair all messy, mouth puffy, eyes still half closed. If I don't get out of this room in one minute, I won't leave."

"What would you do?"

"*Stop*." The deep resonance of his sexually frustrated tone made goose bumps rise on every inch of her skin. "Go back to sleep. When you wake up, go next door to Jiya's house. I've already asked her to give you a ride home. Will you do that for me?"

No help for it. She felt like a cherished belonging and it was…amazing. Mostly because Olive was pretty positive if she asked Rory to do anything, he'd do it. To make her happy. She wanted to make him happy, too, and all that was required was getting home safely. Letting him take care of her in this one way. "Yes. I will."

"Thank you." His shoulders lost their tension, his hand lifting to cup her face. "I'm on the beach all day, but I'm not bartending tonight." Green eyes fell to her mouth and darkened. "Can I see you again?"

Olive wanted more than anything to be back in his arms. As fast as possible. Not being in them *right now* was awful. "I have a study group tonight, but I can miss it—"

"No." The set of his jaw was resolute, but his eyes were soft. "Don't miss school work because of me. How about I give you a ride to class tomorrow morning?"

Butterflies rushed into her chest, wings flapping wildly. "That sounds perfect."

He caught her mouth in a hard kiss that wanted—so badly—to become more. They breathed heavily against each other's lips for a few seconds, Olive's thighs shifting beneath the bedclothes, which Rory obviously noticed, if his groan was any indication. "How does your body feel, sunbeam? You hurting from what we did?"

"No." She kissed the side of his chin. "No."

His eyes closed briefly, then refocused on her. "I'm sorry about the video."

"It's okay." Olive's lips wobbled into a smile. "I searched for you on social media. So I guess we're just even now."

Rory reared back a little. "You did?" He regarded her with a mixture of amusement and confusion. "I'm not on any of that shit, baby."

"I know." She lifted her chin. "It's very frustrating."

"Why?"

"Are you serious? It's like a…virtual footprint. How else am I supposed to learn about you?" She arranged her features in a horrified expression. "*Talking?*"

Rory tickled her ribs and she sheet dropped from her breasts.

He yanked it back up with a bark of pained laughter, covering her up once more. "Jesus *Christ*, if dicks could cry, mine would be sobbing right now."

When he seemed to be debating whether or not to leave, Olive knew she had to help him. He wasn't letting her miss study group and she wouldn't let him shirk his new managerial obligations. As much as it *hurt*. Like seriously, *ouch*. "Go," she managed, saying a silent apology to her newly awakened femininity. "You have to go prep the bar. I'm…" Her breath caught a little as the truth tripped out. "I'm really proud of you for taking on new responsibilities. I'm proud of you for not fighting last night…I'm just proud of you. But you don't have to earn me. I'm right here." She laid a soft kiss on mouth. "Do it for yourself. *You're* worth the effort."

"How'd I find you?" His gaze cut away, a muscle in his throat working. "I guess I have no choice but to go to work now." They shared a frustrated laugh as he rose from the bed, pulling on a shirt that had been laid out on his dresser. Before he could leave the room, his hand paused on the doorknob, Rory looking back at her over his shoulder. "I'll see you tomorrow, right?"

Olive nodded. "I'll be waiting."

"Yeah, still trying to believe it's real," he said, walking through the door and closing it carefully behind him. "Bye, sunbeam," she heard through the barrier between them.

She must have sat there for fifteen minutes without moving. How could Rory be so polarizing and such a comfort at the same time? Her skin was overly sensitized, as if enveloped in static electricity. Her nipples were in tight peaks, as if in denial that he'd left. Finally, she lay down, turned on her side and took a deep inhale of his scent, letting it carry her back to a fitful half sleep. Groans from last night peppered her mind, memories of Rory's mouth between her legs, his arousal sliding home inside her, one inch at a time. How he'd lost control at the end, driving into her hard, saying things into her neck she would have thought crude, but were perfectly paired with a man at the end of his rope. A man she cared about. Desired.

Still half asleep, Olive turned on to her belly and slipped a hand between her thighs. She found her clit with two fingers and worried the nub in fast, tight circles, breathing erratically into Rory's pillow. His scent only got her to the precipice faster.

We fuck, you come. It's a given, you understand?

She muffled her moan, her hips grinding down on to her fingers. Almost. *Almost.* God, she would have done anything for Rory to walk back into the room and thrust himself inside her. Hard. *Hard—*

The storm broke and Olive sank her teeth into her lower lip, limbs shaking as the orgasm rolled through her like thunder, so intense that her calf muscles were immediately sore, her throat strained from trying to stay quiet. "Oh m'God." She turned over and stared up at the ceiling, proverbial canaries circling around her head. "That has to be some kind of record."

Olive sat up and looked around, fanning her skin to cool the dappling of sweat. She didn't know about the rest of the house, but Rory's room was pretty tidy. There were some articles of clothing discarded on the floor—hers included—but there were no dust bunnies running around. He had a calendar hanging on the wall by the door, notations beginning two weeks ago, and her heart tripled its pace, just imagining him going out and buying organizational supplies. Wanting to do better.

She got out of bed and dressed in her clothes from the night before, crossing to the dresser so she could look at the one framed photo in the room. It was the three brothers standing on the stoop in order of height, a laughing woman Olive assumed was their mother holding a pizza delivery box…and a serious man staring at them through a window in the background.

Last night, they'd talked about Rory's mother, but not his father. In fact, was it her imagination or had he tried to *avoid* the subject of his dad?

Olive shook off the odd thought. They had plenty of time to talk about everything. And there was *a lot* to discuss. Olive still didn't know what had provoked Rory in the fight that sent him to prison—and everyone seemed determined to safeguard that information. Which, unfortunately, only made her want it more.

Before Olive left the room, she ran her index finger over the lid of the laptop. Which video had he been watching? With a swallow, she started to lift up the screen, but stopped herself. These videos that made so many people happy only reminded her that she'd been abandoned.

Her gaze couldn't help but drift back to the picture of Rory.

Abandoned. *He* wouldn't do that to her…again. Would he? Not after last night. After they'd found their way back to each other and proved it was too difficult to stay away. *I just want to earn you.* Olive held on to Rory's words on her way to the house next door. And when her phone lit up with a text message from the man himself—*I miss the hell out of you, sunbeam*—she straightened her spine and shoved the foreboding aside.

You've fallen in love. Stop worrying and enjoy it.

But the fear had already built a nest in the back of her head.

CHAPTER THIRTEEN

Rory let out the breath he'd been holding when he saw Olive waiting outside her building, staring down at the open book in her hands. She was gorgeous in the early morning sunlight, her blonde hair lit up with a halo. Such an angel. She smiled, big and open, when she saw his bike approaching, stowing the book in her bag, and his throat cinched up. *Fuuuuck.* He wasn't going to get used to this. The anticipation that had been plaguing his gut since leaving her in his bed yesterday was replaced by trepidation this morning while he got ready.

Wouldn't it…*couldn't* it take the smallest thing for her to get over him? His old-ass house. His work schedule. The fact that he didn't make a ton of money. All of it combined. She was an eighteen-year-old girl. Fickle, right?

Then he saw her and remembered. She's not like anyone else. She's Olive.

A snapping connection reeled him closer, so wild and tangible, he almost forgot she was standing outside of an expensive doorman building. Wearing a backpack. Those things were just enough to remind him of the vow he'd made to himself. No more staying away. God, no. But if she ever decided he wasn't the best man to make her happy…no matter how much he was willing to bust his ass and try…he'd figure out a way to leave her alone. Even if it killed him.

For now, though? For now, he wasn't going to take a single

second of having this girl in his life for granted. In the short time he'd known her, she'd inspired him to see himself differently. Made him ask the hard questions. *What am I capable of?*

Little by little he was finding out.

He'd taken to heart what she'd said yesterday morning. About taking on more responsibility and improving his situation for himself—and it made a lot of sense. He was going to work on that, but it was hard to do a goddamn thing at the moment without attributing it to his need to be a better man for Olive. Maybe he'd get there eventually. Rory didn't know. He just needed to get his hands on the girl who hadn't left his mind for a single second since yesterday. Hell, for *weeks*.

"Hey." Rory stopped at the curb and took off his helmet, setting it down beside the one he'd brought for Olive. In one quick movement, he climbed off the bike and strode toward her on the curb. "Hey. You want to be my girlfriend?"

"Yes."

His mouth crushed down onto Olive's, his forearm slinging beneath her butt to draw her up onto her toes. Commuters honked as they passed by, but Rory barely heard any of it. He was only there for the little whimpers in Olive's throat, the rasp of her bare thighs against his jeans. Their mouths wrestled, Olive gripping the collar of his shirt, not only receiving the kiss, but giving it back to him, like she'd been hungry for it, too. More than his next breath, Rory wanted to pick her up by that tight, sexy ass and feel the life-affirming sensation of her thighs locking around his waist, but he heard the doorman clear his throat at the building entrance and somehow managed to lift his head.

"H-how…am I supposed to go to class now?"

"You'll manage." Rory flicked a glance over Olive's head and noted the disapproval in the man's expression—he was doing nothing to hide it. Olive stared to follow his line of sight, but Rory caught her chin and planted a final hard kiss on her mouth. "Come on. I set up the bar early and bribed someone to cover my chair for the first hour, so I can drive you back."

Just like the other night when Rory rode Olive on his bike, he was a nervous wreck for the entire ride to Stony Brook, but she seemed to sense his tension. The fingers splayed on his chest moved in soothing circles while they ate up the distance on the highway. She planted a kiss in the center of his back and laid her cheek over the spot toward the end of the ride. After that, he wanted to drive another hundred miles, but he wouldn't let her miss class.

They were early, however, which led to them parking behind the Burnbaum building to wait. Rory took off both of their helmets and hung them from the handlebars, but when he would have lifted Olive off the bike, he only turned her sideways on the seat, running his palms up her thighs. Letting his fingertips creep under the hem of her white shorts.

"You were wearing these the day I met you."

"I know," she whispered. "I have a test today, so I wore them for good luck."

How was he supposed to stop himself from devouring her when she said things like that? As it was, he couldn't keep his hands from memorizing the texture of her legs, her arms, her neck and face. She did the same to him, scrubbing her palms on his abdomen, trailing her fingertips up and across his chest.

"So I'm your girlfriend now?"

For as long as you want to be, sunbeam. "That's right."

Pink blew across her cheekbones and he almost proposed. Honest to God. "What exactly does this entail? Having a boyfriend."

"I don't know what having a boyfriend entails for other girls. I only know what it's going to mean for you." Rory tangled a hand in Olive's hair and tongued her lips open, savoring her gasp before sinking them both into a kiss that made the ground move under his feet. "I'm going to want to know you're safe. All the time. I'm going to be obsessive about it—and I don't think I can help that." He pulled back an inch. "I'm going to miss you when you're not with me. When you are, I'm probably going to stare at you. A lot. I'll be wondering how the hell this smart, funny, sexy girl is all mine." He set the hair wrapped around his knuckles free, dropping both hands to her knees and easing them wider so he could press closer, watch her eyes widen when his cock met the seam of her shorts. "I'm going to touch my girlfriend all over." A roll of his hips made her eyelids flutter, her chest shudder. "And I'm going to fuck her rotten."

"Rory," she gasped.

"What's it going to mean for me?" he asked her in between soft bites of her neck. "Having a girlfriend."

Olive stuttered her way through some gibberish, then appeared to give up, scooting her hips closer to the edge of the seat. "I can't think right now."

Unable to subdue his smile, Rory caught her full lower lip between his teeth and tugged. "You want me to get on Facebook? So you can tag me in pictures and all that nonsense?" As soon as the suggestion was out of his mouth, he wanted to take it back. What if she didn't want her college friends to know she was dating a bartender without an education? "Forget I said that—"

"No." She gripped his shoulders, pleasure blowing across her features. "Would you really do that? I know you think social media is stupid, but...I don't know." She seemed to be searching for the right words as Rory held his breath. "I want my profile to say In a Relationship with Rory Prince. Don't you want that?"

His heart started to sprint. "You really have to ask me?" He cleared the rust from his throat. "Do we have time to do it right now?"

"Really?" Olive squeaked, hopping off the bike and whipping her phone out of her backpack. "Oh my gosh, this is going to be so fun. I can't even remember what it's like to set up a Facebook account. I've had mine since I was eleven."

Rory leaned back against his bike and watched her fingers fly over the screen of her phone, her lip caught between her teeth. Given the choice, he would have stood there for the rest of the day telling her the answers to question like, when is your birthday? Where did you go to high school? He got the feeling she skipped over some of the questions about college, but nothing could ruin this chance to make her happy. With something as small as throwing his picture up on a website, no less.

Olive shifted in her sandals. "Relationship status…"

"Worshipping Olive Cunningham."

Pink climbed her throat. "That's not one of the options," she said softly, not quite hiding her smile. "But I like it."

"Good. That's my plan."

They stared at each other for a few beats, the air around them thick. "So. Okay, we need a profile picture."

She lifted her phone, preparing to shoot, but Rory shook his head. "I want you in it."

"Oh."

Olive turned and raised the phone again and Rory saw them on the screen, a study in contrasts. In the forefront, she smiled broadly, wreathed in sunshine. Meanwhile, he was buried in a shadow with his arms crossed, watching her underneath the hood of his eyelids. Before he knew his own mind, Rory snagged Olive around the waist with his forearm, dragging her back against front. On a whimper, she snapped the picture while his mouth moved up the side of her neck—and he couldn't help it. He looked dead straight into the camera and let every man who'd see it know. *Touch her and regret it.*

"Holy whoa," Olive murmured, looking at the final product and making a few, final taps on the screen. "I'm only going to sneak a thousand looks at this during class."

Rory laughed. "Go, sunbeam." He pushed off the bike and kissed her forehead, settling his hands on her hips. "I'll be here when you're done."

She nodded. "Thanks for doing this. I know you have to get to the beach."

"I love doing this." When she started to look hypnotized by his mouth, Rory turned her around and smacked her butt lightly to get her moving toward the front side of the building. As soon as she was out of sight, he blew out a shaky breath and adjusted his hard dick. As much as he'd wanted Olive all to himself, he'd never be the reason she missed class.

Christ, being responsible was fucking painful.

Attempting to take his mind off the ache between his thighs, Rory left campus and gassed up his bike, grabbed a coffee and read the newspaper at a diner. While he was sitting there, his phone buzzed with an incoming text from Andrew.

Need a head count. You coming to Mom's party or what?

Rory drummed his fingers beside his coffee on the counter. Of course he was going to say no. He always said no. As usual, that memory of her disappointment in the courtroom smoked into his head and occupied it. The other memories followed close behind. Coming home from prison and finding she'd aged a decade in the space of two years. Hollow eyes, lines of misery around her mouth. The way she winced when she moved.

The phone creaked in Rory's fist. He had to say no to the party. He couldn't look his mother in the eye after abandoning her to such a horrible fate, could he?

He could if Olive was with him.

Fuck, it was possible he could do *anything* if Olive was with him.

Before he could stop himself, Rory pulled up the text conversation with Andrew. *Yeah, I'll be there. Me and Olive.*

A full minute passed before Andrew responded.

I'm glad, man. You belong there.

With a knot in his throat, Rory paid for his coffee and left the diner. His pulse wouldn't slow down on the ride to campus, his blood buzzing with the decision he'd made. Was it nerves or something else? Something like optimism?

That optimism only spiked when Olive exited the door of the building, smiling and surrounded by girls, her books hugged to her chest. The world moved in slow motion as she searched him out, her lips spreading even wider when she spotted him and pushed her glasses higher on her nose. *Jesus.* What incredible new reality had he been dropped into?

She said a few more things to her friends and nodded, jogging in his direction. He was only partially aware of Olive's friends observing him like a strange new species at the zoo and giggling because Olive's tits were bouncing around, making him hard as iron all over again in his jeans.

"Hey," she greeted him breathlessly, cinching her tight body up against him and sighing, as if having their bodies pressed together restored her. Rory could relate, because he felt the exact same way. Olive was the embodiment of mouth-to-mouth resuscitation. "Everyone is going to that pop-up carnival on the boardwalk tonight." She dropped a sweet kiss onto his mouth. "We should go."

Rory kissed her mouth long and hard. "You want to go, we'll go."

She laid her head on his chest. "I want to go everywhere with you."

And riding back toward Long Beach with the girl he'd never dared dream about clinging to his back, for once it seemed like nothing could go wrong.

CHAPTER FOURTEEN

OLIVE INHALED DEEPLY of buttered popcorn scent carrying on the warm summer night breeze, barely stopping herself from throwing her arms out and dancing in circles like a lovesick lunatic. Already her friends were way too curious about Rory, but the grin she couldn't seem to wipe off her face amplified their interest tenfold. There was definitely a part of Olive that wanted to disclose every single detail of the man who'd sent her freefalling into a giant, mushy love pie. But there was a bigger part of her that wanted to maintain the secrets. Keep them all to herself, bundled to her chest like the softest pillow.

She walked along the boardwalk with Leanne and two other girls from her study group, trying not to be obvious about scanning the evening crowd for a tall man with wind-whipped dark hair and a smirk. Seriously, it had only been six hours since he'd dropped her off outside her building. Why did it feel like a millennium since he'd growled questionable things into her ear and kissed her mouth? She was a windsock in the breeze, flapping around, and she wanted to wrap herself around his solid, grounding presence.

After he'd walked her to the front door of her building, she'd floated upstairs in the elevator, knowing there was a wistful smile plastered to her face. She'd studied, made lunch, dozed off on the balcony in the sunshine dreaming of a wicked half-smile and soulful eyes. When it was time to get dressed for the carnival, she'd taken her time shaving, lotioning, straightening her hair, applying makeup. Putting on the exact right dress, a soft yellow strapless sundress that fluttered at the tops of her thighs. All the while, her stomach flip-flopped and she continually found herself staring into space, almost burning herself with the straightening iron on more than one occasion.

Obviously she hadn't been finished staring into space because Leanne's elbow caught her in the ribs now, sending her hurtling back to the present; a loud, crowded boardwalk.

"Damn, Olive," Leanne laughed. "Your expression is going to get us all pregnant and I'm way too young for kids. Side note, I'll be too young when I'm forty. Kids smell."

"I mean, we all saw homeboy today. It's understandable," said one of the other girls with a playful smile. "But I don't want to be *that* friend who hates you out of jealousy. Just be warned that I'm dangerously close."

Olive pressed her hands to her cheeks. "Sorry, guys. I'll probably be back to normal soon. Right?" When they all passed her skeptical glances, she winced. "Uh, so...what did you guys think of the lecture today—"

"Shut up," Leanne said, giving her a withering look before nodding at something beyond her shoulder. "Rory is over there."

A chemical change washed over her, her skin sensitizing, breath shallowing. Even her earlobes and toes started to tingle, as if preparing for a full-body awakening. And it happened as soon as she turned and saw Rory prowling toward her on the boardwalk, one hand in the front pocket of his jeans, the other pushing through his wet hair. Had he just come from the shower?

Olive's thighs snapped together and squeezed, her sex already softening, growing damp. Her fingers twisted in the short hem of her dress, which she was regretting now. How was she supposed to hide her body's reaction to Rory? If she turned wet upon merely seeing him, a kiss would turn the insides of her thighs moist.

"Hey," he said gruffly, stopping in front of her.

And she'd been wrong. It didn't even take a kiss to make her thighs slick.

When her greeting emerged as an incoherent whisper, Rory's eyes filled with amusement. "Uh oh." He leaned down and rolled their foreheads together. "Looks like you missed me. Maybe even half as fucking much as I missed you."

Olive's knees almost lost power, but her desire to keep their mouths close gave her the strength to keep standing. "I'm trying not to be that girl who gets a boyfriend and ditches her friends. Help me."

His laughter puffed against her lips a half-second before he kissed her, light and tender, but so potent she swayed toward his broad chest. "Something to drink, ladies?" Rory said, throwing a brief glance over her head.

"Beer," Leanne said without missing a beat. "Beer sounds great."

Rory shook his head but didn't take his eyes off Olive. "Nice try. You're getting sodas." He pressed his mouth to Olive's ear. "I'll make you a white Russian later."

Heat propelled into her belly like a torpedo. "Okay," she said, wetting her lips. "What am I going to make you?"

"Happy."

He ran a hand over her hair and backed away, reluctance in every line of his rangy body. "Go have fun. I'll find you."

A moment later, he'd been swallowed up in the crowd's current, although his dark head was still visible above the majority of the carnival goers. Olive watched him go, already regretting her plea for help so she didn't neglect her friends. Still, his willingness to comply when they were both obviously dying to be alone? It made her *like* him even more. Like the unselfish man he was. Even if she had an intuition that he'd be selfish later to make up for the delay. God, she couldn't wait for him to be selfish with her.

Her friends walked up, flanking her on either side.

"Just do it," Leanne muttered.

Olive squealed. Honest to God *squealed*, turning heads of passersby.

"Thank you. I just had to get that out."

"Understood," Leanne returned.

They continued walking and chatting, taking a right into the carnival entrance, which led them just off the boardwalk, where the rides had been erected in a large plot of empty land. Darkness had fallen completely, the blinking, rainbow assortment of lights turning everything in their path into a dreamy kaleidoscope. The smell of salty ocean air mingled with the scent of funnel cake, the crowd a moving sea of animation. Exhilaration danced over Olive's arms, like she was walking inside an electrical current, her laughter coming more freely than it ever had.

"So how did you meet Rory?" asked one of the girls from study group.

"He rescued me," Olive answered, trying not to let her eagerness to talk about Rory show. "I was reading and walking at the same time…"

All three girls nodded in total understanding.

"And I was just about to step into the path of a speeding bus. But he pulled me back." She tucked some hair behind her ear. "A-and then a couple days later, he rescued me from drowning. I got caught in the rip current."

Everyone had stopped walking, their jaws halfway to the ground.

Leanne's expression was one of pure betrayal. "I'm only finding this out now?"

"I was embarrassed! Sorry sorry sorry." Wincing, she gave Leanne a quick hug and continued weaving her way through the crowd, encouraging the girls to follow. "So yeah, that's how we met. And then we took a weird break. But then he had to save me again from a bar fight…"

Olive trailed off, feeling a crease form between her eyebrows. Had Rory really saved her *three times?* Wow. Stringing all those events into a few sentences made her not only seem kind of pathetic and accident prone, but for some reason a niggle of discomfort was crawling up her spine now. She'd wondered since the beginning why Rory seemed so infatuated with her. She was a shrimpy bookworm with a gap between her front teeth who couldn't even legally buy alcohol. He was drop-dead gorgeous and cool and caring and *loyal*.

He was guilty, too. Carried so much guilt, in fact, the weight was practically visible on his shoulders. *If I'd been there, I would have saved her.* Hadn't Rory said that? Was he drawn to Olive because she'd needed saving? The way he hadn't been able to do with his mother?

Now that she *didn't* need constant saving…how long until he lost interest?

The carnival sounds around Olive grew muffled, her friends' conversation fading away until she could only hear the dull thudding of her own heart. A cavern opened in her stomach. Or maybe it had never sealed up in the first place. After the first time she'd been disregarded by her parents for not being exactly right.

Olive felt a hand on her waist. Breath warmed her neck and a familiar voice broke through the haze that had descended.

"Hey, sunbeam." Concern was thick in Rory's tone. "Look at me. What's wrong?"

A roller coaster trundled past overhead at top speed and a group of children ran by laughing, propelling the world back into its usual rhythm. At first there was only the outline of Rory's head, surrounded by blinking lights, but he steadily came into perfect view, worry creasing his handsome face.

"*Baby*," he said urgently.

"I'm fine," she said, then cleared her throat and attempted to be more convincing. "I'm fine. Sorry, I guess I zoned out."

Olive looked around to find three of her friends sipping their sodas grudgingly, but none of them seemed to have noticed her trip to La La land. She wanted to question Rory. The words were right there on the tip of her tongue. Am I just a rescue mission? Using her to fulfill a regret from his past made sense, didn't it? Her psychology professor would call it repression. Or something equally fancy.

"What's wrong?" he said, moving closer and wrapping her in body heat. "Tell me."

"Nothing is wrong, I just..." The suspicion was bad enough—she didn't need confirmation so soon. And what if she was wrong? The electricity between them wasn't a fluke. Or a product of the past. It was right now and it was consuming. *Stop overanalyzing and live in the moment.* "Take me on a ride?"

As soon as Rory smiled and twined their fingers together, the fears began to dissipate. It had been nothing more than a weak moment. This man was nuts about her. It went both ways and she wasn't going to get buried beneath a checklist of how their relationship could go wrong.

"Let's go," Rory said, kissing her knuckles. "I'm stealing my girl," he called to her friends. "Enjoy your non-alcoholic beverages. We'll catch up with you in a little while."

"There are supposed to be perks when your friend dates an older man," Leanne shouted over the noisy carnival. "I want my perks!"

Rory and Olive shared a laugh, settling the chaos in her belly once and for all. He led her to the Ferris wheel, where thankfully there was only a short line. And when Rory wrapped his arms around her waist and rested his chin on top of her head, she wished it would move slower so they could stand that way for longer. Minutes later, Rory helped her onto the moving seat and slid in beside her, pulling down the bar and testing it, not relaxing until it was secure.

He threw an arm along the back of the seat, moving close until they were pressed together from shoulder to knee—and Olive had no idea if his proximity or their sudden ascent into the sky caused the ticklish, weightless feeling in her stomach.

"Hey," Rory breathed against her mouth.

"Hey," she murmured back, letting him ease her lips open with a kiss. A rush went through her, amplified by the air that blew across her bare shoulders, whipping her hair around. There was so much vulnerability in having her feet dangling dozens of feet above the ground while this man's mouth wreaked havoc on her senses, she had to grip the metal bar where it rested at her waist or risk floating away.

After a too-short time, Rory ended the kiss and Olive realized they'd paused at the very top of the Ferris wheel. Gone was Rory's earlier concern. It had been replaced by nothing short of lust. For her. With a bunched jaw, shallow breath and the wind throwing his hair in ten directions, he was nothing short of magnificent. The endless sky full of stars spread out behind him, making the moment bottomless, no beginning, no end. His gaze fell to her chest and he uttered a husky curse, the muscle of his thigh flexing alongside hers.

"God, Olive, I just want to get my fucking hands on you."

Fevered and filled with sudden mischief, Olive arched her back, feeling the neckline of her strapless dress tug low, so low, revealing an indecent amount of her breasts. "Touch me."

The growl that broke from his throat sent her thighs slapping together in their signature move, and that was before Rory's right hand swallowed up one of her breasts, squeezing it once, then rubbing his palm in a chafing circle around and around her peaked nipple. Olive let out a cry, turned on by everything at once. Him, mainly, of course. His touch, his hunger for her, his scent, their attraction. Having her breasts exposed at the top of a Ferris wheel turned her wild, reckless, hotter than she ever thought possible.

She leaned up and teased Rory's mouth into a quick, wet kiss, then leaned back to watch his expression change as she slipped a hand beneath the hem of her dress.

His nostrils flared. "What are you doing?"

Biting down on her bottom lip, she tucked a finger inside her panties, using the gathering moisture to fondle her clit. "Touching myself," she whispered, her words threading together with the wind. "I did this in your bed yesterday morning. After you left."

A shudder rocked Rory, shaking Olive, too. "Excuse me?" He leaned in quickly, their foreheads meeting and rolling together. "You played with your pussy in my bed? Is that what you're telling me, baby?"

"Yes."

"Why?"

"It smelled like you," she gasped, grinding the pad of her

middle finger against her clit, rubbing it rapidly. Faster, faster. "You were around me, everywhere…the second b-best thing to having you on top of me—"

"Enough. *Please*," he begged through clenched teeth, his hands working her breasts, his fingers pinching her nipples and making lights blink in her vision. "*Dammit.* I came here to be your boyfriend. Buy you cotton candy, hold your hand and treat you like the little sweetheart you are. Now all I can think of is…"

"What?"

Rory caught her right nipple between his knuckles and clamped down hard. "I want to drag you into the shadows and fuck you filthy."

Oh my God. Yes. Olive felt the bolts tightening in her tummy, her thighs beginning to writhe on the fake leather seat. But before she could climax, the ride jolted, beginning to move again. Rory cursed again and tugged up the top of her dress, hiding her breasts from view once more. As soon as he finished the task, he snagged Olive's wrist, removing it from the space between her legs, catching her mewl of protest by moving his hot mouth over hers.

"Take me somewhere," she said, looking him in the eye.

A shadow passed across his face, but he gave a tight nod. And no sooner did the Ferris wheel let them off was Rory guiding her out of the carnival. Hand in hand, they climbed the steps onto the boardwalk, dodging the lively crowds spilling out the beachside bars and restaurants. Olive's pulse went ninety miles an hour in her ears. Sticky warmth coated the insides of her thighs. Every pulse point in her body hummed like mini generators and they were all pulsing for this man who she trusted to lead her anywhere. So much that when he hopped the boardwalk rail and held his arms up, she had no doubt he would catch her.

Olive jumped, landing in his arms. Up against his hard chest, so reassuring, but so sexual in the way it flexed, inviting her to rub her sensitive breasts on him, twine her legs around his hips as they walked. She didn't even care where they were going—Rory would keep her safe and he would satisfy her, *thank God*. Ever since meeting this man, her body was relentless in its need to be satisfied. It was an urgent quest now. She required Rory to survive. The erection wedged, thick and hard, between their bodies told Olive she wasn't alone.

She was needed, too, and it was glorious.

They'd only been walking for a matter of seconds when Rory walked them beneath the boardwalk, into the darkness, footsteps pounding above their heads. His heart pounded, too. Olive heard it as she slid down his body, his mouth attacking her from above before her toes touched the sand. And Jesus, *his hands*. They were under her skirt, inside the back of her panties, kneading her bottom with so much potent need, she felt dizzy on the receiving end.

"Tell me to calm down," he rasped between kisses. "Tell me to bring you home and do this right. It should be right for you every time."

"I love this. I need it."

"*Olive.*"

She went down on her knees, her fingers tangling together in her clumsy attempts to unzip his jeans. The move was unplanned. She'd never gone down on someone before, but the desire to drive him past his breaking point was suddenly so strong, so undeniable, she couldn't deny it. Rory tried to drag Olive back to her feet, but she wouldn't go. "Please?" That single word stilled his actions, but his expression was pained. "I want to so bad."

His hand drifted over the crown of her head. "Let me get on

my knees for you instead."

Olive had managed to drag down his zipper while he spoke and she rubbed her cheek now against his hardness where it strained inside his boxer briefs, making him hiss a breath. "You've done it for me every time."

Strong fingers threaded through her hair, shaking but hesitant. "S'because I'm addicted to the flavor you keep between your thighs," he said, voice deep, words slurring. "If I could get away with licking it even more, I would."

Her core throbbed at his words. "My turn," she murmured, easing down the waistband of his briefs, exhaling in a rush when he sprang free. Huge. Heavy. Long. Knowing Rory would pull her off the ground if she showed the slightest hint of trepidation, Olive wasted no time wrapping both hands around Rory's wide root and guiding the head of his arousal to her mouth. She licked around the smooth dome and let him slide into her mouth, over her tongue.

"*Christ*," Rory grated, his fingers tensing in her hair. "Oh God, baby. S'*good*. Oh God."

The praise met her ears like a caress and sent her confidence soaring. She stroked him with eager hands toward her mouth, marveling at the way his flesh swelled with every tight pull of her fists, a hint of saltiness sliding down the back of her throat. So many textures to memorize at once, the abrasive hair of his inner thighs tickling her cheeks, his calloused fingers scraping her scalp, the ridges of his cockhead gliding over the tip of her tongue. The way her throat rebelled when Rory started to flex his hips ever so slightly, introducing his insane hardness deeper than it had gone before.

"Too much? It's too much. It's too much." His words ran together, hips stilling, his stomach shuddering and hollowing inside his T-shirt. "Olive. Sunbeam. I'm so grateful. I'm grateful for every fucking inch you get in that pretty mouth, baby. Swear it." Another earthquake rumbled through him, more of that salty taste finding the back of her throat. "*Fuuuuuck.* You have to get up soon. I'm going to lose it."

If he thought begging would make her stand up, his plan backfired. Watching her boyfriend lose his grip on control was fast becoming her favorite pastime. It turned her nipples to aching spears and amplified the ache between her legs, her wet center quickening and releasing, as if seeking the part of him she eagerly sucked on with her mouth, loosening her lips on the way down and making them *tighttighttight* on the way back up.

"Son of a bitch. *Enough*." In conflict with his words, Rory's hands covered hers, squeezing, stroking, both of them pleasuring him now. "Get up. Get up, turn around and lift your skirt before I blow anywhere but that pussy."

The sand under her knees had nothing on the grit of Rory's voice. It was biting, new, exciting. She'd snapped his tether and wanted to know what happened next. So much that she stood up too fast and went lightheaded. Rory caught her mid-sway, holding her with one arm wrapped around her middle, the other still busy on his erection. They looked down, watching the desperate tugs of his swollen inches, breathing fast together. As if reading her mind and knowing she'd regained her equilibrium, Rory turned Olive toward a wooden post and intuition had her bracing both hands on the rough wood, whimpers falling from her lips, anticipation running amok through her senses. Her body.

"Please please please," she said, hoping he would hear her over the foot traffic echoing from above. "I need you. Now. *Now*."

Rory's mouth pushed against her ear from behind, the sounds

of a condom wrapper ripping audible among the muted boardwalk roar. "Told you to lift your little skirt."

A sob caught in her throat, one hand dropping from the post to scramble back to grip the material and drag it up to her waist, the other remaining braced on the wood. Night air kissed her bare backside, and an instant later, Rory was jerking the thin string of her thong to one side and dragging the smooth tip of his arousal through her soaked feminine folds. He didn't stop, letting it travel over her back entrance, jolting her with surprise, excitement, but she needed him inside her now. Needed that intense joining like she needed her next breath.

"You're down too low, baby. Stand on my boots," he said, grazing her neck with his teeth, the swollen length of his hardness continuing to drag up and back through the moisture he'd coaxed, making just enough contact with her clit to frustrate her, drive her lust to a fever pitch.

Needy, hungry, Olive took two quick steps back, boosting herself up onto his boots and elevating herself those crucial few inches. She'd only managed to brace both hands on the post once more when Rory drove into her with a growl. He caught her scream with the palm of his hand—*Pumping. Hard. Four. Times*—as her cries turned into a strangled plea for more.

"I'm sorry," he said gruffly, his hips smacking against her backside as he thrust into her again. Again. "I'm sorry I fuck you like a woman when you're still half girl. I can't help it."

"Don't help it," she whimpered into his palm. "Don't stop. *Never stop.*"

He let out the groan of a suffering man into her shoulder...and then he braced his feet wider in the sand, taking hers along with them. Leaving her legs spread wider. So wide. Leaving her flesh impossibly open and vulnerable to the thrusts he inflicted, one after the other. His forearm wrapped around her hips and jerked them back so he could grind upward, into her constricting wetness, and Olive dug her toes into his boots, pushing higher, tilting her hips so she wouldn't miss one iota of the incredible impact.

"You're so deep, Rory." Olive didn't recognize her own voice. It was hoarse and gasping and vibrating. "It's so deep. *So deep.*"

"I'd get deeper if I could." He drove into her and held, held, his hand dropping from her mouth to play with her clit. "I'd get deep enough to become a fucking part of you so you don't ever forget me."

Her thighs started to tremble, the glow of her climax growing brighter, rendering her incapable of doing anything but fighting for it. Encouraging it. She wanted to pull apart his words, but the urgencies of her body were too much of a distraction. *Almost there.*

Rory took another sidestep, opening their shared stance even wider, and one thrust later, Olive cried out into the backs of her hands where they gripped the post. "*Rory.*"

"You almost have me convinced I can be a good guy. Every time," he rumbled into her neck, his teeth razing her, his mouth sucking until she gasped. "Then you spread your tight, young thighs for me and I show you, don't I? That I'm always going to fuck you like I've already earned a place in hell." His teeth sank into her neck and he thrust hard, lifting her toes from their perch on his boots. "Might as well enjoy it."

Olive climaxed with her feet dangling in the air and a scream trapped in her throat. She shook so hard under the force of the pleasure that her teeth chattered and her vision dimmed, before erupting with light. Light so intense she threw her head back on Rory's shoulder to avoid it. His fingertips still toyed with her clit, extending the bliss, making it never-ending. But the feeling went from life-changing to nirvana when she sensed him getting closer, too. She needed him *with* her. Experiencing the same exhilaration. Always. Always.

He made a choked sound and she mimicked it as natural as breathing, ordering her inner walls to seize around him, instinctively knowing how to make his peak better. Rory staggered one step to the right, bouncing her in short upward drives of his hips, creating punctuations of Olive's whimpers—and then heat bloomed inside her, Rory's broken shout music to her ears. Her feet dug into the sand as he let her down, her arms closing around her, their bodies swaying, mimicking the ebbing and receding of the ocean.

Without turning around, she could already sense the thoughts running through his head. He was worried he'd been too rough, too explicit, too everything. She only needed to turn around and show him her dazed, satisfied expression to ease his fears. But she literally could not move. Never wanted to move. So she leaned to the right and kissed his bicep, whispering, "Stay at my place tonight?"

Tension left him, reminding her of a wave rushing back to the sea. "I have a condition."

A line formed between her brows, some of the worries from earlier in the evening trying to break through her bubble of contentment. "What is it?"

Before she knew his intention, Rory tossed her up into his arms, righting her askew glasses with a nudge from his nose and carrying her from beneath the boardwalk against his chest. "I want to see the famous matching shower curtain and towels."

She tucked her face into his shoulder and laughed. "Done."

Was it possible to fall asleep while being carried by her boyfriend through a sea of people on the boardwalk? Olive was preparing to test the hypothesis when Rory's muscles turned to concrete. Enough that alarm shivered through Olive, her eyes flying open. She followed his line of sight and found a man staring back at Rory, appearing stunned and uncomfortable. They were roughly the same age, but the man was fair-haired and clean cut, where Rory was a beautiful storm cloud, always ready to throw a bolt of lightning.

"Who is that?" Olive asked.

Rory's Adam's apple rose and fell. "That's him," he said, turning on a heel and carrying Olive in the opposite direction from the man. "That's the man I put in a coma."

CHAPTER FIFTEEN

When Rory was seven, his father decided it was time he learned to swim. His mother had already put Andrew and Jamie through swimming lessons, but money was too tight to do the same for Rory. The sun had been blistering that Saturday afternoon and the community pool was packed so tight with locals trying to cool down, you couldn't see the cracked, concrete bottom through the abundance of bodies. He could still remember standing at the edge, sweat rolling down his spine, wishing Jamie and Andrew weren't at a birthday party. Wishing they'd come along, so he wouldn't have to be alone with their father. He hadn't spoken the entire way to the pool and it was anyone's guess what mood he was in.

"What are you waiting for?" Rory's father's voice came from behind him. "I don't have all day, kid. Jump in."

Rory hadn't bothered reminding the man he couldn't swim—he already knew. Already knew that he'd only ever waded into the ocean up to his knees. What he didn't know was that fear of the unknown scared Rory most of all. Would the water weigh him down? What would it be like to float and not be able to find the bottom with his feet? None of these questions could be voiced out loud, though. He'd be called a sissy boy. Or he'd simply be scoffed at. Maybe even pushed in before he was ready. No, he didn't want that. He wanted to make sure he had time to gather a big breath.

Rory had closed his eyes, inhaled until his chest hurt and jumped into the pool, hoping his body would know what to do. Wishing his brothers were there. The cool wrapped around him, the soles of his feet touching scratchy concrete, and he'd propelled himself to the top, fighting through the panic in his mind, ordering himself to paddle his hands, the way he'd seen Andrew do. *Kick. You're supposed to kick, too.* The first sound he heard upon breaching the surface was his father's laughter. The outline of him had been shadowed, his stocky body outlined by the summer sun—and he'd been holding back the alarmed teenage lifeguard.

"Well done, kid," his father had said, clapping slowly. "We might make a man out of you after all."

Treading water and trying to keep the panic off his face, Rory remembered the unwanted pride that stole through him. He'd pleased his dad. Had that ever happened before? Jumping first and asking questions later had become a theme in his life after that day.

Right now, though? For the first time since the day he'd hurled himself into the community pool…he wasn't jumping first and asking questions later. Not with Olive. When he found her, he'd wanted nothing more than to devour her. Keep her all to himself. But he'd stepped back, hadn't he? He'd given her space to make sure he was the right man. He'd started the lifelong journey to improving himself. Staring back at that man on the boardwalk fifteen minutes ago, he hadn't felt like an escaped animal. Every time he'd imagined running into the person he'd attacked, that's how he assumed he'd feel. Like he should still be in a locked cell. But he had a new confidence in himself tonight—and it had felt damn good.

So good that he didn't want to keep the past locked inside

anymore. As he helped Olive off his bike and they walked toward her building, his pulse ticked loudly in his ears. What would she say if he told her everything? Already he knew the conversation was inevitable, her silent curiosity speaking volumes, but that didn't mean he wasn't nervous as hell to recount the night he acted like an animal. The night he was put away for the safety of the community.

When they were a few feet from the entrance, the doorman stepped to one side, holding the door open. Just like the last two times he'd encountered this guy, the doorman's expression turned distasteful at the sight of Rory—and his confidence dipped momentarily. The guy had every right to regard him like a miscreant. Hadn't he just fucked his sweet, beautiful girlfriend in public—hard and from behind—like the depraved asshole he was?

Olive tightened her grip on his hand and smiled up at him, though, and Rory remembered how she'd sighed into his chest when he picked her up. How she'd begged and gone down on her knees willingly. Eagerly. No, she'd been right there with him. He needed to respect that she knew her own mind, this incredibly intelligent girl.

Her smile dipped when she saw how the doorman sneered at Rory, her mouth opening in an outraged O. "Mike, this is Rory. He's going to be here. A lot." She leaned into Rory's side and passed through the entrance, her chin raised. "We bid you goodnight."

As soon as they were in the elevator, Rory let out the laugh he'd been holding, and Olive joined him. *"We bid you goodnight?"*

She pressed her palms to her pinkening cheeks. "Oh God. It seemed appropriate in my head, but then I just sounded like the dad from *Mary Poppins*."

Rory pulled her into his arms, his body still shaking with amusement. "It was cute."

Olive tilted her head back to meet his gaze. "That's not the first time he looked at you like that, is it?"

Reluctantly, he shook his head.

"You should have told me." She ran her hands up his chest, over his neck and into his hair. "It's not okay. He doesn't even know you."

The elevator slowed to a stop and Rory swallowed. "You don't know all of me yet, either. Is that something you really want, sunbeam?"

She knew he referred to the truth of the night he was arrested. Her solemn expression made that obvious. "Yes. I do."

When the metal door slid open, Olive took Rory's hand and led him into a carpeted hallway with sconces on the walls and apartment numbers engraved on golden plaques. He was glad to see the cameras located on either end of the hallway. It meant she'd be safe. Which meant he'd sleep soundly at night. The tight security didn't make him feel any less out of place, but he focused on the hand inside his. How she gripped him so tightly and continued to throw reassuring looks over her shoulder, as if to say, *you belong. You're here because I need you.*

Rory took a deep breath…and made the choice to believe her.

Olive stopped outside the door at the north end of the hallway, sliding her key into the lock and letting them inside. She flipped on the light and the first thing Rory saw was books. So many books. They were color coded and arranged on shelves, stacked on tables, in piles on the floor. Swanky or not, this place had Olive written on every inch of it. So he felt nothing but comfortable as he entered, following her lead and kicking off his shoes near the door.

He watched as she flitted from room to room, turning on lights and toeing stacks of books out of the way. She cleared paperwork off her kitchen table and looked at her reflection in the stainless steel refrigerator, patting down little flyaway hairs and fixing smudged eye makeup. They traded a laugh when she pressed a few buttons on her laptop and the sounds of Sting's voice singing "Fields of Gold" filled up the apartment. Watching her set the mood was so fucking enjoyable, he had to tear his attention away to take in the rest of the apartment.

Straight ahead was the connected dining room and kitchen, which she'd painted a sunny yellow, two vases of daisies perched on the counter and table. Her Freud towel was drying over the back of a chair, and she'd left a half-drunk mug of tea beside an open textbook. To his left was a small living room, complete with a big trunk that doubled as a coffee table—and a suede couch, a pillow that looked as if it came from her bed on one end. That room led to a balcony with a view of the beach that had Rory whistling under his breath.

"You don't even need to walk to the beach to visit me," he said. "You can probably see me from here."

"Nope. I've tried," she returned, swinging around the kitchen's partition wall and sliding toward him in her socks. "The up-close version of you is better, anyway."

He leaned down and brushed their mouths together. "Yeah?"

"Yeah." She studied him, as if trying to gauge his reaction to the expensive apartment. Rory smiled back, letting her know he didn't give a shit where they were, as long as it was the same place. "Come on," she murmured, pleasure softening her features even more. "I believe you requested a shower curtain and towel viewing."

Watching her tush sway on the way down the short hallway,

Rory made an appreciative sound. "On second thought, maybe that can wait."

He reached for Olive, but she evaded him with a giggle, dancing into the bathroom and flipping on the light. "May I present proof of my adulting skills."

Rory craned his neck to peer into the immaculate bathroom…and dropped his head forward on a chuckle. Her shower curtain was a retro version of Belle from Beauty and the Beast. The cartoon character was naked—except for some well-placed books—and the towels were the exact shade of the purple streak in her hair.

"All right, baby, that's pretty cute." He slapped off the light and tugged her out of the bathroom, kissing her as they swayed down the hallway. "But if you've got Disney characters on your bedsheets, we might have a problem."

She nibbled her bottom lip. "How late is Bed Bath & Beyond open?"

Rory narrowed his eyes.

"I'm kidding. They're a tasteful heather gray."

"Phew."

There was another balcony attached to her bedroom, he saw, when the glow from her bedside table lamp was turned on. He went over to inspect, unlocking and sliding open the door to find a deckchair wedged in the corner. "You sunbathe out here?" He stepped outside and turned in a circle, noting how many other windows looked out onto that exact spot. "Ah, baby. You're trying to kill me."

"What?"

Don't be a possessive asshole. "Nothing." He looked back to find her sitting on the side of her huge, fluffy bed, complete with furry throw pillows. So soft and sexy and female in her pretty dress and the muted lamp light. "I can't help wanting to be the only one who looks at you." He reentered the room and advanced on her, loving the way her eyes raked over him, her body reclining slightly on the bed, as if she couldn't help lying down for him. "I want you to know I've never been jealous. Not in my entire life. It's all for you, so it's…strong."

"You don't want me in my bathing suit on the balcony?"

"I want you to do it, even though it makes me crazy." He stepped between her thighs and eased her all the way down onto the bed. "Don't give me too many inches, okay, sunbeam? You'll tempt me to take a mile."

"I can do that." Her breath caught as he lowered the side zipper on her dress and tugged off the garment, leaving it on the end of the bed. "Jesus Christ," he muttered, staring down at perfection in panties and glasses. Nothing *but* panties and glasses. He trailed his fingertips from her neck, down between her bare breasts, circling them around her belly button. Watching her stomach hollow. "You're the most beautiful thing I've ever seen, Olive Cunningham." Rory stripped off his T-shirt and scooped her up, placing her in the center of the bed and setting her glasses out of harm's way. Leaving his jeans on so he wouldn't be tempted too soon, he dropped down beside her onto his back, stacking his hands underneath his head and staring up at the ceiling. "If I never brought up what happened tonight on the boardwalk…who we ran into…would you ask me?"

"No, but it would kill me," she whispered, running her fingertips up and down the center of his chest. "Just like you can't help being jealous, I can't help being curious."

God, it felt good lying with her there in the near-dark. Talking, touching, no fucking time limit. It wasn't going to be an easy telling, but he would never be more comfortable unburdening himself than he was there, with Olive, in that moment. "Thanks. For letting me get here in my own time." They traded a long look that made his heart squeeze. "The night I was arrested..." He tried to clear the discomfort from his throat, but it wasn't going anywhere. "I was walking home from the Hut. Right there along the boardwalk, where we were tonight—and I couldn't get a hold of Jamie. We were supposed to meet up for a beer. It's not like him to flake. He's always on time, always got something sarcastic to say when I show up late. But I was on time that night and he wasn't there."

Rory knew he was lingering over the insignificant details to delay what was coming, so he forced himself to push ahead.

"I went to Jamie's assigned chair, thinking maybe he'd stayed late because some kids were still swimming—and I saw some older guys. They were in the water. Looked like they were wrestling or something, so I started to head back up to the boardwalk, but I heard one of them say Jamie. Say my brother's name." Rory closed his eyes and tried to breathe through the anger that heated his blood. All these years later, he couldn't control it. "That guy we saw tonight. He was holding Jamie under the water."

Olive's skin turned icy against Rory's and he instinctively turned and gathered her into his arms, rubbing circles onto her naked back, grateful for the job. It was a distraction from his leftover rage.

"They were letting him back up to breathe. They weren't...I don't think they were planning on drowning him. But they were drunk. I could tell that a mile away, could hear it in their voices. They could have made a mistake, you know? And there were *five* of them. Five on one." His chest felt like it was caving in. "I've always been a fighter, baby, but I've never fought unfairly like that."

"No, you wouldn't." Olive held him tightly, her face pressed into his neck. "You wouldn't do that. I know that about you."

"No. But I would keep hitting someone long after they passed out. I did." He let out a shaking exhale into her hair. "His four friends couldn't pull me off. I was an animal. I might have turned on them, too, if the cops hadn't shown up. Wrestled me off." He swallowed hard. "I could have killed him. I think I would have, Olive."

She lifted her head and looked at him, sympathetic and trusting and sad...and he had to get out the rest. Had to get it out before he accepted the comfort he'd never expected and didn't deserve.

"The guy I attacked...Jamie was the first man he'd been with. And I don't know, he regretted it. Or hated that he *didn't* regret it. But he had some alcohol and decided to take out whatever shit he was feeling on my brother." He breathed in, breathed out. "What I did to him usually comes with a much longer sentence, but Jamie testified in court. Told the judge he could have...he..."

"He could have been killed," Olive finished for him, a hitch in her voice. "It's true, Rory. I don't think you can let anger make decisions for you. Fighting and injuring someone is never the right answer, but...just hearing you tell the story makes *me* so mad, I'm not sure I wouldn't have reacted the same way. I'm not sure *anyone* could help it." She gathered him close and he let her, let the fact that she knew everything and still wanted him sink in. Christ, the relief of that made him dizzy. "They could have killed your brother. Seeing that kind of thing happen right in front of you, it's no wonder you weren't in your right mind."

He nodded. "I only remember pieces. Even now."

"Good. I'm think I'm glad you don't remember every detail,"

she said, smoothing his eyebrows with her thumbs. "Thank you for telling me."

She brought their mouths together, kissing him softly and Rory made a rough sound. "Dammit, Olive. This shit is too heavy for you. I hate that I put any of this in your head." He tunneled his fingers through her hair. "You should only hear and see and feel good things."

For several beats, she only regarded him quietly. "The best endings come after a bad start. Good is only good if you've seen enough bad to appreciate it."

If Rory hadn't fallen in love with her at first sight, it would have happened right there, lying in the center of her bed in that ritzy as hell apartment. He was so fucking deep in love with her, he was never going to reach the bottom. The rest of his life would consist of sinking, down, down, down, further into love with this girl. Olive. His Olive.

"Talk to me," he rasped, running his palm over the valley of her side, resting it on her hip. "Tell me about school. Tell me about the last book you read. I want to hear about every second you spent away from me today."

She snuggled closer, the peaks of her tits pressing into his chest hair, and Rory stifled a groan. "Um, okay. While I was in class today, I...was in deep, *deep* concentration—"

"Good girl."

"—listening for your bike engine to come back."

"Ah." He tucked his tongue into his cheek. "Shit. Sorry."

"No, you're not."

"Nope, definitely not."

They shared a quiet laugh, their bodies pressing closer, her bare feet tucking between his calves, her warm pussy resting against the bulge behind his fly. *Hell and heaven fucking collide.*

There wasn't a chance of Rory keeping his right hand from sneaking over her hip to grip that sweet, little butt, molding it in his palm.

"Um." Color stained her cheeks. "The last book I read was called *You Are a Badass*."

Rory raised an eyebrow. "I didn't see that coming," he drawled. "Did you find out you already are a badass?"

"Yes. But it never helps to learn new tips and tricks."

"Maybe." Rory used his grip on her backside to grind her against his lap, taking her mouth in a no-bullshit kiss. When he freed her mouth, he was pleased to find her panting. "Look, Olive. I know I've had some issues with you being so young."

"Really? I didn't notice."

"Quiet, badass." He slapped her tush and swallowed her resulting gasp with his mouth, drawing her into a kiss that had them both moaning. "Yeah, I made your age into a problem, but I want you to know…it isn't one, anymore. You moved here alone, set up this place exactly how you wanted it. You're going to school and making friends. You're killing it for any age, sunbeam." He kissed the tip of her nose. "Am I allowed to be proud of you?"

"I'll allow it," Olive said haltingly. "It's really nice, actually. Having someone be proud of me." She paused. "I know I should be grateful to my parents…the channel allows me to live in a place like this and go to school without worrying about loans, but sometimes I think I'd wish it all away just to hear them say I'm doing a good job."

The sadness in her voice shredded his insides. "I've never had a whole lot of money, Olive, but I know there's no amount that could replace time with you. Proud of you? I'm blown away. As far as I'm concerned, you got here on your own—and thank God you did." He swallowed. "My family can be yours. Me, Andrew, Jamie, Jiya. You've already got me, but there's an us, too, when you're ready."

"Thank you." Olive blinked a few times, dipped her head and lifted it again. She smiled, slinging a leg over Rory's hips and straddling him. "Now this," she breathed, looking down at him from beneath weighted eyelids. "…is badass."

"Oh yeah?" he asked, following her lead and changing the subject, because he sensed she needed to. "Depends what you do from up there."

He lifted her with his hips—and Olive let out a yelp of pain.

Rory jackknifed, his heart firing up into his throat. "Oh my God. What happened?" He ran his hands over her body, searching for injury, his pulse drumming in his ears. "Please tell me I didn't hurt you."

"No, it's fine." She clasped his face between her hands. "It's fine, it just turns out…well, I wasn't expecting it, but I'm just a little, uh…sore. Tender. Down there."

"Jesus." He scrubbed at the pain in his chest, but that only made it worse. "Wait here. I'm going to go throw myself off the balcony."

"Would you stop it?" She laughed, pushing him back down onto the bed, locking their lips together and gradually pressing their lower bodies together. As if he wasn't consumed by enough guilt, his cock reacted to the warm pressure of her pussy like a fucking torpedo preparing to launch. "It's just a little sore, but…I still want you," she murmured, gently rolling her hips. "Really bad."

Rory twisted his fingers in the sheets and waited for his eyes to uncross. "Are you sure, sunbeam? You're not just saying that because I'm hard? Because I hate to break it to you, it's like that any time you're around." He waited until she met his gaze. "We don't have to do a damn thing. I will lie here and hold you. It'll be more than I could ever ask for."

"Really not making me want you any less," she whispered, right before unzipping his jeans and tugging the denim down, along with his briefs, leaving them bunched at his knees. When she crawled back up for a kiss, Rory kicked his garments the rest of the way off, greeting her with his tongue and lips. He didn't know whether to lose himself in the taste of her mouth or marvel over the gorgeous tits swaying above his chest, the thighs moving restlessly on the outsides of his. Mostly, more than anything on the planet, he just wanted to get her off. Because she needed it.

"Baby," he managed in between long, drugging kisses. "I don't have to be inside of you. To make you come." He reached down and fisted his cock, moving it up and back between her thighs, cursing over the slickness between her folds. "Rub your little clit on me. Enjoy my cock. It's there for your personal use."

A shudder wracked Olive and she fell forward onto his chest, her hips shifting as she found the exact right angle…and Rory watched with satisfaction as her eyes rolled back in her head, her hips beginning to pump, sliding her pussy up and down his swollen cock. "Rory," she choked out. "Oh God. It's so sensitive."

"Lean into it, baby. Nothing wrong with that." He gave her bottom a light slap. "*Grind*."

With their gazes locked, Olive did as he instructed, dropping forward to moan into his shoulder, but she didn't press down enough to muffle the sound, and he hoped everyone in the surrounding apartments heard it. Heard his girl taking her orgasm. From him. It was *his* fucking job and everyone would know he did it well, whether they heard her whimpering as they walked down their fancy hallway or spotted her in the elevator with a dazed expression on her face.

"Oh. *Oh*." She threw her head back, mouth open, her hips busy, busy, moving faster. "I'm going to. I'm going to."

"Good girl. Give your wet pussy what it needs."

"I am. Y-*you* are."

"Who, baby?"

"*Rory*."

It took her another few seconds to come, and Rory had to fight to stay still while she rode up and back on his length, tucking her thighs back and rubbing her clit on his dick like she would die without the friction. Sweat formed on his upper lip, his chest, his brow. If his hands wrapped around the sheets any tighter, he was going to rip them to shreds. His balls throbbed, the same thick tempo echoing in his head. *Don't move. Don't move. She's going off...*

Rory actually shouted when she hit her peak, it was so hot to witness. She bore down on him, trembling violently, eyes blind. "*Goddammit*, how can you be so beautiful?" Rory gritted out, flipping her over onto her back and standing above her on his knees, cock in hand, stroking himself at the pace a man only hit when he neared the end and wanted the agony over. She panted below him in the sheets, her belly directly below the erection he jacked off, her blonde hair spread out around her like spilled paint. "You look like a fucking angel, but I'm going to come all over you, anyway. Going to mark what's mine."

A look of wonder crossed Olive's face, as if she'd only caught on that he was out of his mind obsessed with her. That wonder turned to innocence as she arched her back and shook her tits for his entertainment and Rory came with a roar, moisture leaving him in white ropes and striping her belly, her breasts, before finally dripping on the ruined thong that covered only a strip of her pussy. Coming that hard twice in one night must have been a shock to the system, because he couldn't get his shaking body under control. It kept up as he found a towel in her bathroom and cleaned her off carefully. And it was only beginning to subside when he fell onto the bed and gathered Olive up into his arms, raining kisses on her hair, her cheeks, her mouth.

"Rory," she said into the darkness. "Will you be here in the morning?"

"Of course I will, sunbeam," he answered, covering her in the light sheet. "I have to prep the bar, but I won't leave without saying goodbye, all right?"

If he'd been more alert or less drained by what they'd just done, maybe he would have noticed how she rapidly deflated in relief. And wondered why.

CHAPTER SIXTEEN

OLIVE HAD NEVER been so warm and relaxed in her life. She usually woke to a distinct sense of woe, knowing she'd have to drag herself out of bed, perform hygienic rituals and slog to class. This morning was another story entirely. She might as well have been floating on a river of golden orbs to the soundtrack of babbling water. Her limbs wouldn't move and that was A-OK with her. Moving seemed totally overrated when Rory had her wrapped in a bear hug and her bare backside was tucked into his lap.

A smile curved her lips as she opened her eyes and stared at their reflection in her hanging mirror across the room. Their size difference and…just plain differences were on full display. He was tall, hard-bodied and covered in ink, dark hair in a messy wreath around his head. Olive was small, paler, fair, not a tattoo to be found. Rory had a possessive arm slung over her middle, his softly breathing mouth lost somewhere in her hair. The hair on his thighs tickled the backs of her legs, and somehow that was a wild turn-on.

What would they do when he woke up? Would he roll her over onto her stomach and just pressssss inside of her hot and slow? She recalled his gruff morning voice from the last time they'd spent the night together and wanted to hear it again, abrasive and urgent in her ear.

Olive closed her eyes and focused on keeping her breathing

even, lest she wake up her boyfriend with horny face in full effect. Although, Rory definitely wouldn't mind. As if his body sensed hers was awake, his erection swelled against her bottom, pressing into the split of her cheeks. Olive mouthed *oh my God* at her reflection in the mirror, her eyelids fluttering at the new sensations. Not only was she waking up in a man's arms, she was waking up beside a sexy, caring, sensitive, magnetic man who she also happened to be in love with.

So in love she wondered if he could hear the rapid acceleration of her heart. The way it rebounded off her ribs like a ping pong ball in a dryer.

I should tell him.

At the very notion, her stomach turned over and the beating of her heart took on a different quality. A nervous one. Before she'd fallen asleep last night, she'd dropped from the highest high, down to an unstable precipice. She was falling deeper and deeper in love with Rory, but the fall only seemed to be making her more scared. More apprehensive over how long he'd remain in her life.

Sure, the way Rory felt about her was in every touch, every kiss and word. But he had his insecurities and the past to overcome. Her heart believed he would come back to her every night. Her head was a different story, though. He'd walked away once. He'd walked away. And if he did it again, after her feelings for him had gone past the point of return, would she survive it?

Needing some air, Olive eased out from beneath Rory's heavy arm, one corner of her mouth edging up as he rolled onto his back, arms and chest flexing as he stretched and went still again. She could have sat there memorizing every inch of him, but she rose instead and threw on an old T-shirt, wanting to get her head on straight before Rory woke up.

Quietly as possible, Olive brushed her teeth, then padded down the short hallway into the kitchen. Upon entering the apartment last night, she'd been so distracted by Rory's presence, she hadn't even removed her phone from her purse. If that didn't prove her infatuation, nothing would, since Olive hadn't slept without her cell charging on her nightstand since she'd bought it in high school.

She found her purse where she'd dropped it on the dining room table and slid out the device, swallowing hard when she saw a text message on the screen from her mother. They hadn't spoken in a week and only in a cursory *how-are-you-settling-in* type of way. Their conversations hadn't been anything but forced in a long time, and every once in a while, Olive sensed her mother wanting to dig deeper. Maybe even apologize for how the family had been divided with everyone on one side and Olive on the other. But it never actually happened. Because of that, every time they hung up from a phone call, Olive only felt worse. Less connected to the people she used to spend every waking moment with.

After a moment of hesitation, Olive slid her thumb across the screen, unlocked the phone and went to her messages.

Hey sweetie! Just wanted to give you a heads-up, in case you watch the new episode. We needed a new toy unboxing space for the channel and your room was our only option. We'll make sure you've got somewhere to sleep when you come to visit, so no worries! Maybe we'll even have a resort adventure next time you make it down here! Just didn't want you to be caught off guard. The new episode is so fun. Gadget Mania! Love you, Mom

The numbness started at the top of Olive's head and spread down, into her belly, through her fingers and toes. She stared at the screen so long, the words started to blur together. Acid crept up the walls of her throat and into her dry mouth, eradicating the minty goodness her toothpaste had left behind. Most of all, there was pure sadness. Emptiness. Exactly how she'd felt the afternoon she'd walked into the house and found them making a video without her. Betrayed. Dumped.

They'd finally erased her for good.

Olive heard the bed creak down the hallway and dropped the phone. Didn't even bother picking it up. She wrung the fingers of her right hand in her left, trying to fix the numbness, but it didn't work. Even her lungs lacked feeling. She couldn't even be sure she was breathing.

When Rory walked into the room pulling on his T-shirt, Olive backed up automatically, her butt running into the kitchen table and jostling the vase of daisies.

"Morning, sunbeam," Rory said in that hoarse morning voice, his head popping through the top of his shirt. "Early class, right? I can give you a ride there, but I can't stick around this time to drive you back." His expression told Olive he was troubled by that fact, but she couldn't process the reason behind it. Couldn't think of anything but the text message. How completely untethered she was now to her family. Officially carved out.

"Y-you know…yeah. I'm, um…I can take the bus both ways." She crouched down on stiff legs and picked up her phone, leaving it face down on the table. "You should get to the bar."

As soon as the suggestion was out of Olive's mouth, she breathed easier. The part of her that wanted nothing more than to spend time with Rory was not in control. Nowhere to be found. And her heart was too bruised to work or stop her. She just wanted *away*. Away from anything else that could cause damage—and Rory had already caused some. Hadn't he?

Yes. Oh God, she couldn't open herself up to get set aside again.

She'd had her head in the clouds. She'd been naïve to think this was forever.

Forever? *Seriously?*

They'd only known each other for a few weeks and he'd broken up with her once already. It was only a matter of time before it happened again. She didn't want the emptiness anymore. The sense of loss inflicted by her parents was terrible, but she'd put herself on the road to living with it. Functioning despite the hurt. Adding the potential loss of Rory was unwise. It would kill her if it happened.

"Olive." Rory's dark eyebrows drew together. He took a step in her direction, but she jerked back again—splashing water from the vase onto the table—and her obvious alarm seemed to skyrocket his own. "Jesus, baby. What's wrong?"

She exhaled slowly. "Nothing."

"Like hell." His concerned gaze ran the length of her, his tan skin turning chalky. "Is it…worse today? The soreness?"

"No, it's nothing like that. It's nothing at all." Having regained a small semblance of her equilibrium, Olive moved behind the table, pinched a napkin out of the holder and mopped up the water she'd spilled. "I just have to get ready for class."

"Good." His eyes stalked her every movement. "I'll wait."

"Rory…"

"What?" He shook his head. "Something's up. You're scaring the hell out of me."

"Me?" Olive scoffed, hating her tone. "I should be scared."

"What does that mean?"

This wasn't going to work. She couldn't tell him the truth. Couldn't tell him about the news from her family. How it had gutted her. Made her realize how foolish she was being to trust him again. He would convince her otherwise. He'd make promises and kiss her and she would be a goner. Even now, his energy across the room was tugging the low muscles in her belly, the complicated ones around her heart. Every part of this man affected every part of her. She just had to make him go. *God, just go, before you make me hurt worse.*

Last night at the carnival, she'd landed on the theory that Rory was drawn to her because she'd needed saving. Maybe he would lose interest the longer she went standing on her own two feet, neglecting to step in front of buses or almost drown. He could get bored. She wouldn't be fulfilling that need to save someone, left over from his bad home life. The abuse his mother had suffered when he was in prison.

To Olive's desperate brain, it all made sense. He wouldn't want her for long. He would leave. He would cut her off, just like her family had done. It would hurt. Too much to survive.

"Rory, I think…I just think…" Olive's eyes landed on the textbook lying open on the table. "I think it's better if I just focus on school right now. I-I shouldn't have ditched my friends last night. They're the people I should be spending time with. People who value the same things as me. School. Getting my education. I can't…this won't work."

If possible, Rory's face paled further. "You're giving me the smart girl look."

Even though she didn't have a clue what that meant, Olive didn't like it. How was she looking at him? She couldn't even remember what she'd just said. "I'm sorry, Rory," she said on a trembling exhale. "I can't."

"Can't be with me," he rasped, his eyes taking on a far-off quality. "Dammit, sunbeam. My gut is telling me to shake you, kiss you, find out why you're scared of me all of a sudden. Is it…it's because of what I told you, right? My arrest—"

"*No.* That's not it."

The denial burst out of Olive, but he talked right over her, seemingly beyond listening.

"I promised myself if you cut me off, I would man up and respect it. Leave you alone," he said, the words sounding raw as cut glass. "My bones tell me to do the opposite, though, baby. I'm standing here and you're in pain for some reason and I don't know what the fuck to do."

This time, it was Olive's turn to not listen. Her heart plummeted at the misery in his voice, but her mind snagged on only one part of his ravaged explanation. *I promised myself if you cut me off, I would man up and respect it. Leave you alone.*

"Did you ever think this was going to work out?" Hot tears crowded against the backs of her eyelids. "Or were you just waiting for a signal to walk away again?"

Rory's gaze sharpened. "Is that what this is about?" He made a rough sound. "If I could go back in time, I would run after you. It *kills* me that I didn't."

Olive could feel herself weakening. She had to press her hip into the table until it hurt to keep her feet from moving. Carrying her in his direction, where she knew he'd pick her up, hold her, take away the ache in her chest. "That's not what this is about." She barely managed to whisper the lie. "I have to get ready for school. I have to do what's best for me. *Please*, just…"

Her throat closed up, refusing to let her say *go*.

Rory filled in the blanks with a desolate expression. "I'll go," he said, rubbing the heel of his hand against the middle of his ribcage. "If you think me leaving is what's best for you, I have no choice." Before she could prepare, he came around the table and moved in close, so close she could feel the kiss of his breath on her lips, the heat of his body caressing her skin. "I'll go, but you listen to me, Olive Cunningham. Go live your life. I hope you believe me when I say I hope you have the *best* fucking life, baby. I want everything for you." In her periphery, she could see his fists clench at his sides, as if he wanted to reach for her but wouldn't. "While you're out living that life, remember I'll be out there somewhere. Living for *you*. And if you want me back for one day—one *minute*—I'm yours. And I'll do it over and over again, no matter how many times you decide this is wrong afterward. I'll wait around to worship you, sunbeam. Any time you want me. Do you understand?" He leaned in and she whimpered, preparing for a kiss, reeling from the vow he'd just made. "I'll love you with this black soul until God tears it out of me."

Even as her heart soared, a voice doubted in the back of her mind. No. No, she couldn't know for sure if he loved her. He might just *think* he did.

Rory started to back away slowly.

I love you, too. Oh God, I love you so much.

Her mind screamed the words at his back as he pivoted and walked out the door.

The silence that descended was so loud, she could hear the dull pitch of the ocean, layered beneath her own wheezing breaths. Common sense warred with the crazy, authentic, untamed love inside of Olive, keeping her rooted to the spot.

He's gone. He's gone, so I can't get hurt.

He's gone, so I'll hurt forever.

It was a losing battle. And in that moment, shaken, lonely, heartbroken and still in shock from what her family had done, she was too weak to fight.

It was late Friday afternoon when Olive realized she'd been

sitting in the student library for...three hours. Really? She'd come in to check out a book and that book still sat in front of her on the polished mahogany table. Unopened. She'd been doing this a lot since Tuesday morning. Zoning out. Forgetting why she'd walked into rooms...or why she'd left the apartment. It was probably better that way, her brain blurring reality and making her surroundings feel like lethargic dreams in which she wasn't actually participating.

Olive opened the book sitting in front of her and closed it again, burying her fingers in her hair, inhaling deeply and trying to block out the stunted sound of her heartbeat. It seemed to follow her every place she went, blaming her for its cracks.

How was it possible Rory had walked out of her apartment three days ago? It could have happened an hour ago, the horrible finality of the moment was so fresh and sharp. And yet, it also felt like it happened nine months ago. She no longer had any frame of reference for time, except school. Get up, get dressed, get on the bus, pretend to listen in class, go home and stare blankly at convoluted notes.

Olive's gaze drifted over to the screen of her phone, noticing the date—and not for the first time. This evening was Rory's mother's birthday party. She'd told him she would go and now it was only hours away. What was he feeling? Had he backed out? God, she hoped not.

Olive was in the process of pushing back from the table, intending to replace the book on the shelf and make her way to the bus stop, but Leanne plopped down at the table with a smack of her gum, earning them an evil look from the librarian.

"Hey you," she said, giving Olive a soft punch in the shoulder. "You're here late."

"Yeah, I know." As she'd been doing all week, Olive forced a smile on to her face that honestly, just felt freakishly unnatural. But it was better than her alternative downer face. "Just doing some reading before heading back to Long Beach. Why are you here?"

"Had a meeting with the guidance counselor."

Olive nodded. "You walking to the bus stop? I'll tag along."

"In a minute." Leanne drummed her fingers on the table, ignoring the exasperated sigh from the librarian. "Tagged you in some pictures on Facebook and you haven't even commented. Are we even friends if people don't witness it virtually?"

"Sorry, I..." Olive snatched up her phone and tapped the blue and white icon. "I haven't been on. I haven't—"

"Been doing much of anything?" Her friend passed her a half-smile. "You've been behaving like a zombie. I was worried our professor was going to use you as a case study. Classic Incurable Heartbreak-itis, wouldn't you agree, class?"

She massaged her forehead with three fingers. "Ugh, we've only been friends for, like, a month, and I've swung between hormonally charged and despondent. No judgment for cutting your losses and running. Seriously."

"Shut up." Leanne nodded at Olive's phone. "Well. Comment, dammit. Get back in my good graces."

"Okay, okay." Olive went to her notifications and saw that Leanne had tagged her in four photos. When she clicked on the first one, her heart went flying up into her mouth. Rory. There he was. Behind the bar in the Castle Gate. He looked...devastated. Crazed, even. Whatever he was looking at had upset him greatly. To the point that Jamie was restraining him. "When did you take this?"

"The night we went out with those senior douches." She shrugged. "I snapped it when we walked into the bar and I recognized Rory from the milkshake shop. That's around the time he saw Zed's arm around your shoulders."

"Oh," Olive said, sounding small. Desperate to see more of the man she'd been missing like an amputated limb, she swiped to the next picture and her stomach took a dive. Taken the day he'd picked her up from school, the photo showed Rory leaning against his bike like the world's most delicious bad boy, grinning as she approached. Olive's pulse turned choppy, that familiar loneliness stealing over her. Shit. Oh shit. She missed him so badly. How had she not fully realized the way Rory looked at her? Like she was…walking on water or something.

Urgency trickled into her bloodstream. As if she needed to get out of there. But she remained in the seat, needing to see another picture of Rory more than oxygen.

It was them in the milkshake shop, sitting in the booth. That very first day.

Olive didn't even have the words to describe the shot. It was…

Love at first sight. No arguments. No denying it.

Rory's jaw was flexed, his green eyes awed. Olive looked like she was trying to catch a mouthful of bees. And they both looked a little scared.

"Wow." Moisture ran down her cheeks. "Y-you take incredible pictures."

"That's what I was talking to the guidance counselor about. I'm switching my major to photography." Leanne smirked to let Olive know she was kidding. "Olive, that fucker is crazy about you. I don't know what happened, but there has to be a solution."

Olive scrolled to the final picture and the breath clogged in her lungs. "When…"

"That afternoon we studied at that outdoor café. Remember?"

Barely. There were bits and pieces, but if she recalled correctly, the study date was the day after she and Rory broke up on the sidewalk across the street from her building. And yet there he was, in the background of the picture, watching her from a distance. He was getting ready to turn and leave, seeming almost exasperated with himself. But there was no denying the absolute yearning on his tired, unshaven face. It was stark and obvious and breathtaking.

"Why didn't you tell me he was there?"

"Maybe I should have." Leanne shrugged. "I'd only seen you guys together once before that day. I wasn't sure if he was stalking you or just…fucking heartsick. Guess I wanted to be sure it was the latter before I encouraged you to get back in touch with him, but that happened all by itself." She flung her arms out dramatically. "Now here we are again."

Olive stared at the picture until her vision blurred. He'd never really left her, had he? To a degree, she'd known that. Known that he'd escorted her bus to school, driven past her building. Having proof that he'd missed her, that he'd never checked out of their relationship…it was powerful knowledge. She'd never truly been abandoned by Rory. Not even for one single day.

Rory's name was highlighted, meaning he'd been tagged in the pictures. After only a moment's hesitation, Olive tapped on it and was taken to his profile. Nothing had changed. He still had the same picture of them behind the school. They were still listed as *In a Relationship*. He probably hadn't logged on once since she'd made the accounts. He'd never had any use for social media…

No. Wait, he *had* been on Facebook. Olive's hand slowly came up to cover her mouth.

He'd checked in at the milkshake shop. Every day since she'd thrown him out.

Oh God. She'd thrown him out of her apartment. Out of her life.

How could she have done that? She was in love with this man. Fierce, unmovable love—and he felt the same for her. Not being in his arms at that very second was agonizing.

While you're out living that life, remember I'll be out there somewhere. Living for you. And if you want me back for one day—one minute*—I'm yours. And I'll do it over and over again, no matter how many times you decide this is wrong afterward. I'll wait around to worship you, sunbeam. Any time you want me. Do you understand?*

Olive stood fast enough to send her chair flying backward. She hadn't lost him yet. She could fix this. *God, please let me be able to fix this.* When Rory told her he would wait indefinitely, she believed him. She *trusted* him. He would never hurt her again.

She would never hurt him again, either.

And she'd start by keeping her promise.

Olive fumbled with her phone until she found the right contact and hit send. "Jiya?" A hum of reservation was her only greeting. Fair enough. Jiya was loyal to Rory, and Olive was grateful for that. He deserved to have people in his corner. Still, thank God they'd traded phone numbers the day Jiya had driven her home from Rory's house. "Can you tell me the address for the birthday party?" Silence passed. "Please?"

A moment later, Olive leapt up from her chair and drew Leanne into a hug. "Thank you for helping me pull my head out of my ass." She squeezed her friend hard. "I owe you big time."

With that, she ran from the library, backpack in hand.

"*I still don't see any comments,*" Leanne called after her.

CHAPTER SEVENTEEN

Rory's hands protested as he turned the bolt connecting the table to its base. He was beginning to strip the metal by twisting the screwdriver over and over, but he was enjoying the strain in his hands. It lessened the pressure in his chest by one percent—and for now, that was just enough to keep him from falling off the deep end.

Finally, he dropped the screwdriver and sat back on the floor. He looked around at the overturned tables. Old ones that used to grace the dining room upstairs but had since been retired to storage downstairs. Every single one of them had been flipped over, the bases detached and refastened, the tops sanded down. He'd been in the basement of the Castle Gate since last night completing the task. The chair legs were next. That might prevent him for another couple hours from going to find Olive. Just to see her. Just to make sure she was all right. Was one glimpse so much to ask?

He buried his head in his hands and felt stickiness oozing from his palms, blood mixed with grease that he quickly wiped on his jeans.

Rory was in hell. How he'd managed to survive since Tuesday without seeing Olive was beyond him. Could he manage it for the rest of his life? No. No fucking way. He had to leave town. If he saw her with another guy, rationality wouldn't be an option. Hell, he was bleeding and sweating in a dark basement—he wasn't rational *now*.

Just like he'd been doing for the last seventy-eight hours, he replayed the scene in Olive's apartment. How she'd been white as a sheet when he'd come out of the bedroom. How she'd jumped when he spoke. He still had a suspicion that *something* happened before he woke up. That he was missing a piece of the puzzle. Still, there was no denying that he'd hurt her. She'd been harboring pain since the first time he'd left—and Jesus Christ, knowing that he'd hurt Olive in any way was like nails driving into his skull. He'd missed it. He'd missed how badly she'd been affected by their break-up. If he'd known, if he'd had a fucking inkling, he would have spent every second reassuring her. Now it was too late.

He'd lost the girl of his dreams.

No, that wasn't right. She was the reason he'd *started* to dream again.

Feeling that familiar constriction in his throat, Rory cleared it hard as he could and snatched up the screwdriver, walking on his knees toward the next defunct table. Before he could begin the exhaustive process of unscrewing the ancient, rusted bolts, the light in the basement came on. He squinted toward the stairs to find Jamie and Andrew at the top, identical expression of *what the fuck* on their faces. When they'd opened the door, sounds from the bar upstairs came flooding in and Rory realized it must be early evening. Jesus, how long had he been down there?

"Hey, man," Andrew said, descending the stairs, Jamie behind him. "We're on the way to mom's party. Stopped by to pick you up."

The party was today? Rory swiped the back of his wrist across his forehead, probably leaving a streak of filth behind. Olive was supposed to go with him to see his mother for the first time in years, but there wasn't a hope in hell of that now. More than anything, he wanted to stay there on the floor, causing himself physical pain to distract from the destruction of his heart. He wouldn't, though.

Olive had woken something up inside of him. The need to be a better man. Not only for her, but himself. That was why he hadn't immediately gotten shitfaced when Olive kicked him to the curb. He wouldn't go back to that. He wouldn't go back to being unworthy of her. Unworthy of respect. Even if he couldn't have Olive anymore, he wouldn't squander the spirit of hope and optimism she'd handed him like a selfless gift. If he squandered what she'd given him, he squandered Olive. And the difference she'd made in him was all he had left of her.

Though it was difficult, Rory braced a hand on the wall and struggled to his feet, his legs half asleep from being in awkward positions on the hard concrete floor. "All right," he said, sounding like his vocal cords had been severed. "Let's go."

Jamie came forward and pried the screwdriver out of his hand, unable to hide his wince at the condition of Rory's hand. "Let's swing by the house first and grab you a shower. Maybe a change of clothes."

"I can't. I have to just go like this. If I stop to think, I'll just stop. I'll just stop."

After a few seconds of silence, Andrew coughed into his fist. "I think I've got some extra shirts down here. They probably say Bud Light on them, but..."

While his older brother rummaged through boxes, Jamie went into the small employee bathroom, emerging with a fist full of wet paper towels. "Don't move."

Rory had been caring for himself out of necessity since he could remember. He'd been the last kid to come along, after the bright, shiny idea of a happy family had gone out the window for his parents. After their relationship had gone from occasionally volatile to strictly volatile. So he'd stayed out of the way, got himself ready for school. Fed himself when necessary. But hell if Rory didn't stand there in the basement of the Castle Gate and let Jamie clean his face and hands while Andrew changed his soiled shirt. He just couldn't do it himself today. Maybe tomorrow.

On the way out of the bar, Andrew stole an order of French fries from the kitchen and ordered Rory to eat them. He sat in the back of Andrew's car now—Jamie in the passenger seat—eating what tasted to him like cardboard out the Styrofoam container. The Revivalists drifted through the speakers, but the windows were down and the rush of the wind prevented Rory from making out the words. It was overcast outside, getting ready to rain and he was glad for it. He wouldn't have been able to stand the sunshine and face his mother, his guilt, all in one day.

Jamie made eye contact with him in the rearview mirror. "You good?"

Rory managed a nod.

"It's going to be fine. You'll wonder why you stayed away so long."

They drove without speaking for a while. "You want to talk about what happened with Olive?"

Jamie sent their older brother a look. "Have I ever complimented your impeccable sense of timing?"

"It's fine." Rory set the fries aside and massaged the bridge of his nose. When was the last time he'd slept? Every time he closed his eyes, he saw Olive backing away from him, so he'd flat out stopped trying. "She gave me the smart girl look."

"What's that?" Andrew asked.

He let his head fall back against the seat, way too exhausted and empty to have the conversation. "She's focusing on school. She needs people around her who value the same things. I don't blame her. I...don't blame her." He swallowed the knot in his throat. "She might have let me try to be what she needed, but...I don't know. I wasn't worth the risk when I'd already left and hurt her. Don't blame her, okay? She's fucking perfect," he finished under his breath. "Just don't let me go see her. I told her I'd let her live her life. If I see her, I'll..."

Jamie turned in the passenger seat. "What?"

"Beg. I'll fucking beg to have her back." He blew out a breath. "She doesn't need that."

It took another fifteen minutes to reach Queens and they eventually turned down the block to their aunt's house where Molly Prince had been living for the past four years. Rory couldn't even remember the last time he'd been there. Probably for Thanksgiving or one of the other holidays they only celebrated casually now. The street had been cleaned up, repaved. Trees lined either side, the same bodega sat on the corner, but it had gotten a new awning. Rain had started falling lightly from the sky now and the windshield wipers squeaked as Andrew parallel parked along the curb.

Andrew shut off the engine and met Rory's eyes in the rearview. "She doesn't know you're coming, so why don't you get your head on straight and come in when you're ready?"

Jaw tight, Rory nodded, grateful for the silence that descended when the car was empty. He'd been dreading the moment he would see his mother again for so long. Now that it was here, though? It wasn't as daunting. Maybe because he'd unburdened himself to Olive about how he'd left his mother to face the abuse alone...and she'd still wanted him. For a little while, only. But that still counted for something. No, it counted for everything.

He could do this. He might be at his weakest today, but overall, he was stronger from his time with Olive. He was a better version of himself. She'd made him take a look at himself in the mirror and realize he didn't want to be lacking anymore. Made him realize he was in control of the future and could move on from the past, little by little.

God, he wished she was there.

Rain started to come down heavier on the roof of the car, signaling an imminent downpour. He already looked like shit and didn't need to resemble a drowned rat on top of his three-day beard and sunken eyes. Better get inside now. After several bracing breaths through his nose, Rory pushed out of the car, not bothering to shield himself from the rain as his long strides ate up the sidewalk. He made it to the end of the walkway leading to the house…and that's where his head of steam started to evaporate. Everything inside him felt so fucking unsteady. Could he really go in there and come face to face with his mother in this weakened state? What if she resented him? Would he be able to handle that when he'd already been cut off at the knees by Olive not wanting him anymore?

The rain started to pick up while he hesitated at the end of the path. *Make a decision.*

His breathing turned choppy, his feet inching backward—

"*Rory!*"

His head whipped to the right. And there was Olive, running toward him down the sidewalk, soaked. Soaked head to toe in sandals and a blue and white flowery dress, looking more beautiful than anything he'd ever witnessed in his entire life. He turned on a dime, his skin screaming for contact with hers—but he stopped short, his hands dropping back to his sides. Why was she there? *Don't hope. Don't you dare fucking hope she came to be with you.* It would burn him at the stake if that wasn't the case.

"Olive," he rasped, feeling like a leashed animal being held back by sheer willpower instead of a harness. "What are you doing here?"

"I..." She took a step closer, pushing wet hair out of her face. "I told you I'd go with you. To the party."

His mind raced, trying to read between the lines. "You came because you didn't want to break a promise?" He shook his head. "That's sweet. That's just like you, sunbeam. But please go home. Don't you know it's *killing* me to look at you?"

"I'm sorry." She covered her face with her hands, then let them drop. "I'm sorry for what I said, Rory. For making you leave. I was wrong. I-I..." A big hiccup left her mouth. "I miss you so much, I can't think or eat or sleep or read. Why are you looking at me like I'm a bomb that might go off at any second? I know I deserve it, but..."

The words *I miss you so much* were winging around Rory's brain like boomerangs. *She missed him. She missed him.* He opened his mouth to ask her what that meant, but it occurred to him in one fell swoop that she was getting more drenched by the second. What if she got sick? No, he wouldn't let that happen. Praying the car door hadn't locked behind him, Rory guided her to Andrew's vehicle and pulled the back seat door handle, breathing a sigh of relief when it opened. "Let's talk in here. I can't concentrate when you're getting wet."

"Okay."

As soon as the door closed, Rory was in a potent combination of heaven and hell. He was near enough to Olive in the back seat that their thighs brushed, but he wasn't sure if she wanted to be touched yet. So he just waited. Waited, breathed and stayed as still as possible so he wouldn't lunge for the girl staring up at him with the most incredible eyes on the planet. The girl he loved so much, he was half-delirious just sharing the same oxygen with her.

Olive's inhale was stuttered. "The morning I asked you to leave, I woke up to a text from my mother. They'd turned my old bedroom into a toy unboxing space. For the channel." Her audible swallow mingled with the rain pelting the rear window. "It was like being abandoned all over again and then I c-couldn't think of anything but the time you left. And how bad it would hurt if you did it again. And I just got so scared." Her fingers twisted in the damp hemline of her dress. "I invented reasons you probably like me, because I was so positive you would stop a-and leave again. Maybe you liked me because you *needed* to rescue someone, because of the time you couldn't." She gave him a meaningful look. "I just needed a reason—*any* reason—to push you away so I could avoid being…dropped. So maybe I am a naïve girl, Rory. Maybe I am. Because being without you is terrible no matter how it happens and I've sped it along." A sob pushed out of her mouth, her body beginning to shake. "And I'm in love with you and you won't even *hold* me now. I've ruined *everything*. I've—"

Rory's arms were around her in a split second, gathering her tightly against his chest and dragging her back across the seat into his lap. She straddled him as natural as could be, their bodies locking together like two halves of a whole. His heart lurched repeatedly, shocked over going from broken to complete so fast, and he pressed a hoarse sound into her hair, running his hands over every inch of her he could reach. Her head, her back, her hips, her face. "Did you just say you're in love with me?"

"Yes," she whispered, nodding. "*Yes*. I'm so sorry, I didn't mean what I said. About needing only people from school in my life. I was *lying*. D-did I ruin this—"

"*Olive*." Every ounce of feeling inside of him—disbelief, honor, relief—went into that single use of her name. His mind raced between every word she'd said, no idea where to land first, returning over and over again to the last part. This girl loved him. She loved him back. Was he dreaming? No. No, the weight of her in his lap was real. She was there. Craving eye contact, he clasped her face in his hands, bringing their heads together. "I love you. *I fucking love you.* I always will. Always. Let's get that straight first."

A shudder passed through her and she sagged against his chest.

"Don't you dare be relieved by that. You think I could stop loving you?"

Looking into his eyes, she shook her head. "No."

"I didn't hold you at first because I would have broken if you were just here to keep a promise. And not because you needed me."

"I'm here because I need you," she said against his mouth, scooting closer on his lap. "I'm here because I need you so bad."

Olive's pussy pressed down, so hot and sweet on his cock and the flesh filled with pressure. That horrible, wonderful weight only she could satisfy. While they breathed against each other's mouths, faster and faster, her hips starting to roll, the rain began coming down hard, turning the back seat into its own private world where they were the only two people who existed. "Look at me." Never taking his attention off of her, Rory dug his wallet out of his pocket and tossed it on the seat, his fingers searching for the square foil packet he kept tucked in the billfold. "Olive, baby. Do you honestly think *I* rescued *you*? I'm the one who was drowning before you pulled me to shore. Look at me, sitting outside my mother's birthday party, someplace I wasn't sure I'd ever find myself. All because you believed in me."

Her eyes were soft and damp, running over his face. "I'm sorry I doubted how you feel."

"No. Don't apologize," he said gruffly, peeling the wet hem of her dress up, up her thighs, bunching the sodden material around her hips. "I just wish you'd told me about the text message, baby. About what they'd done. I'm so sorry. It's hard for me to understand how someone could know you...and not want to keep you close as possible. It makes me feel so fucking helpless because I can't fix it."

"I don't need you to fix anything for me," she said, brushing their lips together, side to side. "Just..."

"Just what?"

She looked down. "I don't like knowing that you were waiting for me to break up with you. That you had some plan to leave me alone, let me live my life, at the first sign of trouble."

Rory understood Olive more in that moment. She didn't want casual. She needed to be secure in the knowledge that he wasn't budging. That his presence in her life was as solid and indestructible. If it took from now until the end of time, he would make sure she never questioned that he'd be standing beside her forever.

Unable to wait another second, Rory teased her mouth into a reunion kiss that escalated quickly, tongues finding each other and mating, heads slanting. Her thighs turned restless around his hips almost immediately, her fingers tugging at the collar of his shirt to bring him closer. And *fuck*, he'd missed those little whimper sounds.

Rory reached down between their bodies and unzipped his jeans, wincing as he pulled out the source of his ache. He covered himself quickly with the condom, pushing aside Olive's thong with the head of his dick, leaving himself positioned at her entrance. But not quite inside. Just pressing, pressing, letting her wetness coat the latex.

"It's yours whenever you want to start riding it," he gritted out, leaning back so he could watch the lips of her pussy part, hugging his cock and sliding down a few inches, Olive working her hips to take him inside, her fingernails digging into his shoulders. "When I'm deep as you can handle me, we're going to have a little talk."

"Okay," she gasped, turning glassy-eyed. "Talk. S-sure."

Rory's heart swelled with love, but lust surged up and demanded attention as Olive's tight pussy rippled and squeezed around the entire throbbing length of him. "Good girl," he managed, finding her taut ass cheeks in his hands, easing her into a rhythm that made her mouth form an O. "That's right, baby. It's a perfect fit." He slapped her bottom lightly, the smack sound echoing in the back seat. "Fuck your man."

"*Rory,*" she moaned, seeking out his mouth for a kiss. He gave it to her and then some, growling deep in his throat as she rolled into a faster pace, learning on the fly exactly how to angle her hips so that sweet clit rubbed on his cock every time she moved. "I'm going to come so fast. I can't help it. Missed you. Need you."

"Time for our talk, Olive." The love inside him expanded to include a little darkness. A lot of possessiveness. Those things had always been there, ready to bleed into the intense feelings she'd stirred, but Rory's instinct rose up and set them free now. To plunder. Because his soul told him Olive needed them. "I'm done being noble. If you ever ask me to leave again," he rasped against her mouth. "I won't. Fucking. Go. Is that what you want to hear?"

Olive's nod was jerky, excitement lighting her gray eyes. "*Yes.*"

He brought his mouth over to her ear, breathing against it. "You'll have to call the cops, Olive. Tell them to bring an army. That's what it'll taken to drag me out. Away from my girl."

"It won't happen. It'll never happen."

"If it does, I'll still come back." He kissed her hard, swallowing her sobs with a greedy mouth. "This is how obsession works. Is. This. *What you need?*"

"*Yes*," she cried out, riding him hard. Fast. "That's what I need, Rory."

"Done." Rory began lifting his hips in sharp thrusts, meeting every twist and grind of her hips, and Olive gasped, increasing her pace, gaining more and more momentum. "Christ, baby. *Baby.* You're getting me off so good." Knowing if she didn't come in the next thirty seconds, he was in danger of peaking first, Rory undid the top three buttons of her dress, pushing aside the wet material to suck her nipples through the thin silk of her bra—and her pussy seized up around him, broken versions of his name filling the car as she shook through an orgasm.

Rory surged up into her tightness one final time and roared, the climax pounding through him with such force, his lungs wouldn't fill for long moments, his vision blurring. There was nothing but Olive and the love overflowing their hearts into the back seat of the car. They clung to each other for several minutes as the rain slowed into a pitter patter, their mouths meeting in slow, meandering kisses, their hearts pounding closely together, as if attempting to merge into one.

"I love you, Olive. My God, I love you so much."

"I love you, too, Rory." She kissed his chin, his cheek, his mouth, resting her cheek on his shoulder with a contented sigh he planned to hear every day for the rest of his life. "Are you ready to go inside?"

"I'm ready for anything, as long as you're mine." He wrapped her in a bear hug. "And we're not just going to see my family. We're going to see yours, Olive."

She lifted her head and gifted him with a beautiful smile. And a few minutes later when they knocked on the door and Rory's mother answered, bursting into tears and pulling him into her arms, he wondered how a man could do anything but succeed with so much love coming at him from two directions. The remaining cracks in his foundation were filled with hope. Knowledge that the future would be nothing but bright, especially when his mother hugged Olive, too, already halfway to loving his girlfriend. As if anyone could help it. Rory vowed to himself that Olive would have a special place with his family. It would be hers, as much as his.

Everything he was capable of giving would be hers.

For as long as he was breathing.

THE END

Want more from Tessa Bailey?
Here's a sneak peek at RUNAWAY GIRL...
A swoony, sexy romance between a gruff, military man and a beauty pageant coach that just ditched her own wedding...

CHAPTER ONE

Naomi

I'M FIFTEEN MINUTES away from marrying the man who ordered me the wrong white wine at our rehearsal dinner last night. There are definitely far better reasons to get cold feet, but the lemony Pinot Grigio clings to all sides of my throat now like a reminder.

He doesn't know you.

I scan my reflection in the mirror, looking for flaws. The smallest thing counts. A flyaway blonde hair, a wrinkle in my custom Pnina Tornai wedding dress, my diamond pendant being slightly off center. But no. I may as well have stepped right out of a bridal magazine. A real life Photoshop job, primped, airbrushed and ready to be shipped down the aisle.

That's exactly what this feels like. I've been packaged. My attributes were all selected from a pull down menu. Pageant queen. Check. Hostess skills. A must for any southern housewife! Writes a mean thank you card. Why, of course!

After all, I'm preparing to marry the next mayor of Charleston. The rest of my life will be lived beneath the finicky microscope of old money and my own peers, who judge twice as harshly. I've been groomed for this my whole life. Cotillion. Finishing school. Private tutors. Non-stop critiques from my mother. I am in this to win it.

But with ten minutes on the clock, I'm not sure what winning is anymore.

What. Is. Winning?

I fall onto a cushy divan—gracefully of course—and force air to enter my nose and leave my mouth. In. Out. In the full length mirror's reflection, I watch my bridesmaids plow through a bottle of champagne behind me, speculating in hushed tones on what my wedding guests will wear to the big day. It's the tip of spring so yellows, blues and pinks are likely to make an appearance. They talk about it like the weather report. I should get up and join them, right? Any second now, they're going to realize I've been quiet too long. I have been quiet too long. Where are my manners? They're here for me. I should be thanking them for their support and handing out their wedding party gifts, but all I can do is think of Pinot Grigio.

I'm a Sauvignon Blanc girl. Everyone knows that.

A little hiccup leaves my mouth, but I disguise it with a polite cough and stand up once more, smoothing creases from the embroidered satin of my dress. I notice my maid of honor watching me with a wrinkled brow and give her a pinky wave, forcing a smile until she returns to a conversation which has now turned to which of the groomsmen are single.

Five minutes. Oh God.

The sick citrus flavor has now traveled to my stomach, stewing and gurgling. I haven't thrown up due to nerves since my first pageant at age four. I won't start now. I can't. This is a thirty-thousand-dollar dress. A vomit stain wouldn't exactly match the beading. And worse, my friends have eagle eyes. They would definitely notice and they would know. They would know I'm panicking. I can't have that. The future mayor's wife is a cool customer. Unflappable. She makes everything look easy. That is who I am. Not a jittery girl with back sweat.

A flash of black outside catches my eye. Not exactly an eye-catching color, but among the pastels, the dark figure crossing the street outside the church draws me closer to the window. It takes me a moment to place the identity of the black-haired woman stomping up the church steps with a defiant expression, but when I do, my feet go from cold to frostbitten.

Addison Potts.

What is my estranged cousin doing at my wedding? Lord knows she wasn't invited. Her side of the family hasn't been welcome at so much as Sunday brunch in decades. I haven't seen her in Charleston since we were in our twenties. Possibly longer than that, since we never ran in the same circles. My circle is currently popping open their second bottle of champagne—and an answering pop happens somewhere in my midsection as Addison pauses outside the church doors. Not hesitating, exactly. Just giving guests a chance to look at her. Encouraging them.

Shaking things up.

A small laugh puffs out of me, creating condensation on the window.

Where has she been? What has she been doing while I prepared to be the keeper of someone's social calendar? I don't know. But I bet whatever she did…she did it for herself. On her own terms. She's been living. That much is clear.

Addison frowns and glances up at the window, but I duck

back before she sees me. My heart beats wildly in my throat. What would Addison see if she looked at me? Exactly what I am. A pampered southern belle with the appropriate amount of friends. An inner circle of four, an immediate network of thirty-two and a broader outer circle of two hundred and fifty. A blonde beauty queen whose interests include scrapbooking, creating signature cocktails for parties and fancy gift wrapping. My long lost cousin would probably laugh at me.

Maybe she should.

When I look back down at the church steps, Addison has disappeared into the church, leaving a stir in her wake. And for the first time in my life, I understand envy. I've never caused a stir. Not once. I've inspired approval. Matching sweater sets don't exactly drop jaws, do they?

"Naomi," calls my maid of honor, Harper. "I promised your mother we'd have you walking down the aisle at three o'clock sharp. We should head down."

A bridesmaid leans a lazy hip against the liquor cart, jostling the bottles. "Yes, let's not cross the woman. I want to make it to the reception with my limbs intact."

Despite the cyclone brewing in her belly, Naomi's tinkling laugh filled the room. "Ladies, would you mind terribly if I had a moment alone with Harper? We'll be down in a shake."

"Of course," chirped three bridesmaids, far too brightly.

What am I doing? This impromptu meeting is not on the agenda. A quick glance at the clock tells me I am now late for my own wedding. If my mother has to come up the steps, she will be breathing fire and that's the last thing I need right now. We don't want to keep Elijah waiting. No. No, we never want to do anything to upset this perfectly perfect ideal life I've landed. This is what I've always wanted. Wifehood to a rich, respected man. A military hero who inspires sighs of gratitude when he walks down the street.

A good man. An honest man who will stay true to his vows. A kind, compassionate human being. That is Elijah Montgomery DuPont, the next mayor of this fine town. He just happens to think I prefer Pinot Grigio. That's only the tip of the iceberg, though, isn't it? I spent hours getting coiffed for the rehearsal dinner last night and he looked right through me. Sure, he kissed my cheek and nodded as I spoke. Made sure I arrived to my assigned seat without injury or assault. I love Elijah.

He just doesn't love me. And after seeing Addison Potts outside on the church steps, I know exactly why. Where my cousin is vivacious and exciting, I'm a cookie cutter, boring-as-beige debutante who's never lived outside of the staunch parameters laid out for her. I haven't experienced anything, unless someone planned it for me. I'm not interesting or worthy of anyone's undivided attention. My fiancé is probably standing in front of the altar right now, dreading the next fifty years of eye-glazing conversation about the country club and charity planning committees.

Me. I'm going to be inflicting the boring.

Oh Lord. No. I can't do it. I don't want to do it.

I have to get out of here. I have to save Elijah.

And, more importantly—I think—I have to go do some living. Just for me.

"Naomi." Harper waves a hand in front of my face. "I've been calling your name, honey. What did you want to talk to me about?"

"I'm not going down there," I whisper, wide-eyed.

Well, now. There it is. My first dropped jaw. "What now?"

My gaze bounces around the room, cataloguing everything I

need to take with me. Purse. My car keys are zipped in the inner pocket. I definitely need those because my suitcase is in back, packed full of honeymoon clothes. As long as I have them, I won't need to go home and risk my mother hog-tying me and dragging me back to the church. I can just…go.

Excitement is building in my chest. I'm really doing this. I should be terrified, but knots are loosening inside me instead. I'm not getting married today. I'm making this choice.

With a shaky swallow, I swish toward the secretary in the corner and scribble out a note with a trembling hand. *I'm sorry, Elijah. I couldn't do it.*

I hesitate before penning the next part. Am I going to completely sever ties with my fiancé? Yes. And no. I need to give Elijah his freedom. It's only fair after what I'm about to do. I can't ask him to wait while I figure myself out. That wouldn't be fair. But I know I could search this entire world and not find a more decent man. So while I'm going to break off our betrothal? In my heart…I'm going to keep hope alive that we'll find our way back to each other. *If we're meant to be, he'll forgive me one day, won't he?*

I didn't want it to end this way, but it's for the best.

Those final words blur together as I stare down at them, until the clock drags my attention away. I'm now ten minutes late for my own wedding. Unheard of. My mother is probably on the way—no, those are her footsteps coming up the stairs now. I have to move.

I shove the folded note into Harper's hands. "I'm sorry to do this to you, sweetheart, but I need you to give this to Elijah." She starts to shake her head. "You've been a good friend, Harper. I wish I had more time to explain, but right now, I need you to stall my mother while I escape down the back staircase."

"But why?" Harper breathes, fanning herself with the note. "He's just so handsome."

There's no time to answer, though, and I turn from my wide-eyed friend, snatch up my purse and jog toward the staircase door. Not easy in my crystal embellished pumps I had designed after Cinderella's slippers—which heavens—seems so trite and cliché now. It's dark on the way down to street level, making it feel like a dream. Or a mistake. I'm not supposed to be in the dark, I'm supposed to be walking down the aisle adorned in refracted stained glass lighting. We tested several different positions of the sun before deeming three o'clock the optimal aisle time. I can already hear my mother grinding her molars. We're losing the sun.

Who cares? I laugh as I throw myself through the exit door and click through the parking lot, purse in one hand, the hem of my wedding dress in the other. There isn't a soul around. No one wants to miss the upper crust betrothal of the town hero and his trophy wife, do they?

While that harsh thought stings like an angry bee, it makes me move even faster toward my white Range Rover, parked in the valet section. I want to be more than someone's blonde Stepford Wife. I want to be…more like Addison. More like the black sheep cousin who walked with her chin up into a church full of people who dislike her. I want to be brave like that. Before that can happen, I need a reason to be brave. I need to see and learn and do.

Go back, says a voice in the back of my head. You can't really be doing this.

You don't have what it takes to survive.

That might be true. But I am doing this, regardless.

I'm a runaway bride.

Within moments, I'm peeling out of the parking lot and gunning it toward the freeway, my veil blowing in the wind. Before I take the on-ramp, though, I pull over and map a sensible route to Florida on my voice guided navigator.

One ditched wedding does not a spontaneous woman make.

After that, though, I'm on my way.

To what?

I guess I'll find out.

Get the rest of RUNAWAY GIRL here: https://bit.ly/2NxXzp6

Want Access to FREE audiobooks?

Have you heard of the Read Me Romance Podcast? It's a FREE podcast, hosted by New York Times Bestselling Authors Alexa Riley & Tessa Bailey, where you'll get exclusive, never-before-heard audiobooks! You can only find these stories on the podcast!

Subscribe for free to get original audiobooks from some of your favorite authors, including Alexa Riley, Tessa Bailey, Claire Contreras, Kennedy Ryan, Alessandra Torre, K Webster, Katee Robert, Kathryn Nolan, Jen Frederick, Skye Warren and many, many more!

A different author will be featured on the podcast every week. Read Me Romance will begin a brand spanking new, original audiobook every Monday, releasing one section per day, until wrapping it up with a big, swoony happily ever after on Friday! All listeners need to do is subscribe to the FREE podcast, so they never miss a chapter!

iTunes
Google Play
Website www.readmeromance.com
Instagram @readmeromance

Made in the USA
Middletown, DE
02 January 2022